Strip for Murder

Strip for Murder

Richard S. Prather

No part of this publication may be reproduced or transmitted in any form or by any means, electronic, or mechanical, including photocopy, recording, scanning or any information storage retrieval system, without explicit permission in writing from the Author.

This book is a work of fiction. Names, characters, places and incidents are products of the author's imagination or are used fictitiously. Any resemblance to actual events or locals or persons, living or dead, is entirely coincidental.

© Copyright 1983 by Richard Scott Prather
First e-reads publication 1999
www.e-reads.com
ISBN 0-7592-1476-X

Other works by Richard Prather

also available in e-reads editions

Novels

Case Of The Vanishing Beauty
Bodies In Bedlam
Everybody Had A Gun
Find This Woman
The Scrambled Yeggs
Way Of A Wanton
Dagger Of Flesh
Darling, It's Death
Too Many Crooks
Always Leave 'em Dying
Pattern For Panic

For
Gene and Marciele Mccoy

Strip For Murder

1

This was a party that Cholly Knickerbocker, in tomorrow's Los Angeles Examiner, would describe as "a gathering of the Smart Set," and if this was the Smart Set, I was glad I belonged to the Stupid Set Not many of the fifty or so guests here — none of them, I hoped — could know I was a private detective named Shell Scott, but few could have avoided the impression that I might have sneaked in here by mistake. I was the only man not in a dinner jacket, and there were even some diplomat-type characters wearing tails.

And here I was in brown slacks and a tweed jacket over a sports shirt called, according to the salesman, "Hot Hula." At least there were no wild Balinese babes doing things on the shirt; it was just colorful. Anyway, this was a warm summer evening, the last day in June, and even if I'd known I was to crash the Four Hundred tonight, I wouldn't have had time to change clothes.

Less than half an hour earlier, a Mrs. Redstone, the gal who was tossing the ball, had phoned me and said that she needed the services of a private investigator, and none other than Captain Phil Samson of Los Angeles Homicide had recommended me. Sam is my best friend — male friend — in town, so I'd told Mrs. Redstone that I'd buzz right out to her home in the

Wilshire district. She would recognize me, she'd said, from Samson's description.

That was all I knew; until Mrs. Redstone latched onto me and made further explanations, I was merely to mingle "unobtrusively" with the guests. That was going to be loads of fun. It was also going to be impossible.

I'm six-two and weigh 205 pounds, have short white hair that sticks up into the air as if a small bleached porcupine were curled up on my scalp, whitish eyebrows, plus a very slightly bent nose. There's a nick in my left ear, a souvenir from a dead hood. He wasn't, of course, dead until right after he shot at me. Anyway, I was pretty unique in this plush gathering, so, without trying to hide, I leaned against a wall, eyeballing people and listening.

One of the biddies near me was yakking about some gal who was "coming out," and I looked around eagerly, thinking maybe this tomato would bust out of a paper-covered cake and the party would get livelier, but no such luck. She was talking about her daughter, who had reached the age of consent — probably about eight years after first consenting — and was having a party so she could be stared at over champagne glasses.

I'll tell you one thing: Neither that party nor this one would be *my* kind of party. I drink bourbon and water, and I like to stare at women over women. There was one woman here worth staring at. A bunch of us solid citizens were scattered around an enormous, drafty room in the enormous, drafty Redstone house, and I leaned against my wall, clutching a bourbon highball I'd lifted from the tray of a thin-lipped waiter, who had sneered at me as if I were the waiters' waiter, and the interesting woman was sitting on a low gold divan a few feet from me.

She was animated, laughing, talking to a guy who sprawled next to her. The guy was completely relaxed, legs crossed, balancing a half-full highball glass on the toe of one black leather shoe, which was even more pointed than his head. He was looking around the room, and he glanced at me momentarily. He frowned slightly, then his gaze passed on. But he kept frowning.

The girl fluffed short blonde hair and said, "Poopy, pay some attention to me."

Obviously the guy was a real blue blood, because a man with even half a dozen red corpuscles would have been paying so much attention to her that she'd have been screaming or surrendering. Her lips were bright red in a milky-white face, and light brows arched over blue eyes. She had a nice body, too, though a trifle slim for my taste, but what she had was all hers for sure. When it comes to clothes, sometimes the more money women have, the more they spend for less, and this gal was wearing so little that she must have been a billionaire. The dress was dark green, strapless, clinging, and almost off. She finally got the blue blood's attention, and while they chatted I looked over the gathering some more.

I didn't know what Mrs. Redstone looked like, but I did know she was pushing sixty and worth about fifteen million dollars. Plenty of millions more were undoubtedly scattered among the guests, but there were some others who weren't high society, just high.

I recognized a male juvenile from one of the studios, so drunk he had his toupee on backward. Next to him was an ex–Miss America. She had a thirty-six-inch bust of which thirty-five inches was back, the sweet, sad expression of a molting angel, and little else — but she was six feet tall and could tap-dance like a fiend. In the same group with them was a guy even bigger than I, a heavy, thick-bodied man I'd never seen before, but he was talking to another character I did recognize. And I started wondering what was going on here.

The guy I recognized was wearing a tux, and he looked peaceable enough, but I knew he wasn't the peaceful type. I didn't know his real name, but in hoodlumland his moniker was simply Garlic. Garlic and the other man glanced at me, then went on talking. Garlic's friend was a stolid, unsmiling type, his face kind of marked up and the coat of his dinner jacket tight over his shoulders. Most coats would be tight on him. He was a vital-type egg, with power seeming to ooze out of him, and I got an impression of a man full of iron and wires and cold-rolled steel bars. Garlic glanced at me again, and I was brooding about what a Folsom graduate was doing here with the well-scrubbed rich when somebody said:

"Hey."

It was a soft, husky voice alongside me. Not a female voice, though. While I'd been looking elsewhere, the blonde's friend from the gold divan had walked up to me.

"Hello," I said.

"What are you doing here?" he asked me.

Only he said it like "Fetch me my spats, boy," with a very nasty inflection. He was a little younger than I, under thirty, dark and good-looking enough in a weak-sisterish way, despite fairly rugged features. He stood about five-ten and glared up at me insolently, lids lowered in boredom over black eyes. His black hair lay close to his head in tight waves.

"Just . . . mingling," I said agreeably. "Nice party."

"How the hell did you get in?"

"I shot the butler," I said. "What makes it your business?"

The corner of his heavy lips pulled down. "I'm Andon Poupelle," he said.

"That's nice. Glad to meet you, Poopy."

A slow flush crept up under his tan. "You make a lot of noise with your mouth," he said. "And you smell like cop to me."

I straightened up, wound my right hand into a fist, and then loosened the fingers again. "Listen, friend. I can make just as much noise with *your* mouth if

3

you want it that way. You can relax on purpose or accidentally, but if you've got something on your mind, tell me nice."

I got a surprise. Poupelle's belligerence left him suddenly. He swallowed and ran his tongue over his teeth. They were beautiful teeth, even and regular as a row of small sugar cubes, porcelain-capped, a translucent white. He glanced at my right hand, still slightly raised, then spun on his heel and walked away from me.

The blonde was alone on the divan now, so I walked over to her. If she was Andon's date, he'd made me mad enough to try moving in. Hell, I'd been planning that even before he'd made me mad. Out of all the women tottering around in here, she looked like the only one who wouldn't go to the Blue Cross when there was a blood drive on, and there was a chance she wasn't social register, just social.

"Hi," I said. "Can I get you a drink, or a mink coat or something?"

She smiled. Nice. Teeth almost as pretty as Poupelle's. And it was easy to see, from where I was standing to where I was looking, that she had things much prettier than anything of Poupelle's. "No, thanks," she said. "You can sit down, though. You didn't look very comfortable there on the wall."

"Ah, then you noticed me."

"I thought somebody had hung a modern painting over there." She grinned, not stuffily at all. "I prefer the old masters, myself."

"How do you know I'm not an old master?"

"Oh, you're not an old anything."

"Sweet. I'll admit these rags are a little resplendent, but I'm trying to set a style. The Hollywood Boulevard fashion plate, that's me."

She shook her head. "Really, did you do this on purpose, or didn't anybody tell you to come dressed for dinner?"

"I'm not going to eat with my clothes. As a matter of fact, I may not eat at all." It was true enough, especially since in my wanderings I had scouted the enormously long dinner table, set with place cards and everything, including printed menus. The menus were in French.

I went on, "I'm afraid to eat. I can't read the food."

She laughed. "I'll read it to you."

"Show-off. You know, one of these days I'll throw a ball for the Smart Set and the menus will be printed in Abyssinian. We'll see how smart they are."

She gurgled a little and we made extremely small talk for another minute. Then she said, "You know Poopy, do you?"

"Not well," I told her. "Well enough."

Either she failed to get my message or else she didn't adore Poupelle either. Anyway, she kept smiling, so I proceeded on the assumption that we were agreed.

"He's so much fun," she said. "So interesting to talk to, isn't he?"

I went along with the gag. "Yeah. Of course, I've had better conversations with parakeets."

She frowned a little. "You mean you don't think he's . . . clever? Intelligent?"

Oh, she was marvelous, completely deadpan, almost as if she were serious. I grinned at her. "That boy could be drowning and he might know he was wet. Otherwise, though, his brain cell is probably — "

Suddenly I discovered I'd been going along with the gag all by myself. The blonde *had* been serious. Her tone was frigid when she said, "Go back to your wall."

"Wait a minute. I — "

"Wait nothing."

"OK, miss." I got up. "Miss what? I should know who I've insulted. Whom. Have I insult — "

She said icily, "I'm Miss Redstone. Vera Redstone." Then she shook her head vigorously. "Oh, damn! That's twice tonight. I'm not Miss Redstone. I'm Mrs. Poupelle. Andon's my husband. We've only been married two weeks, and I keep getting my name — What am I telling you this for?"

I sat down again. "You mean you're Mrs. Redstone's daughter? And — *his* wife?"

"Yes."

"Well," I said. "Him. You must have been talking about Andon. Why, he's — he's a prince!"

It wasn't any good. "Go back to your wall," she said.

Well, what the hell, I don't mess around with guys' wives, anyway. At least, not when they've only been married a couple of weeks. I got up again, and somebody tapped me gently on the shoulder.

I looked around at Garlic's face. Looking at Garlic's face, all of a sudden and up close like this, was a very unpleasant experience. In naming this lad, his underworld chums had shown a complete lack of ingenuity. Nobody would ever forget why Garlic was called Garlic, not if they ever got this close to him. I almost suffocated.

"Hello there," he said gently.

I exhaled, put my index finger against his chest, and pushed gently. He stepped back a little and said, "There's a fellow would like to talk with you outside."

"Who?"

"Me."

"Go on out and wait."

"Uh-uh. Come on."

I looked down at Vera. At Mrs. Poupelle. Her nose was wrinkled in distaste. "Who invited this ape?" I asked her.

She looked briefly at me. "I don't know. Mother made out the guest list. So she made two mistakes."

I walked over to my wall again and leaned on it. I was tired of this party and I wished Mrs. Redstone would show up and claim me. Garlic tagged along. "You comin'?"

"Get lost, Garlic." We'd never met before, but I'd seen him around. Just as I knew his name, it was a foregone conclusion that he knew not only my name, but also that I was a detective. Most hoods in the L.A. Hollywood area know me because I've sent several of their circle to the poky or to Forest Lawn, which is a cemetery.

"I'll level with you, Scott. I must ask you to blow. You destroy the funeral tone of the establishment."

"Funereal."

"Uh-uh. Funeral." He grinned and breathed at me. "Let's go." He latched onto my left arm.

Talk about funerals, this evening was beginning to pall on me. The empty highball glass was still in my right hand, so I lifted it up on a level with my chest and said, "Please let go of me fast, Garlic."

He had a lot of strength in his fingers, and he squeezed my biceps until it hurt. I took a fast look left and right. Nobody was eying us. Then, as Garlic increased the pressure to ease me toward the door, I dropped the highball glass, pointed all four fingers straight out, and jabbed them into his neck. My fingers hit his Adam's apple just as the glass bounced on the carpet. A funny squeak came out of his throat, and I knew not much else would be coming out for a little while. His face got red and he balled both hands into fists as I bent over and picked up the glass, keeping my eyes on him.

I cupped the glass in my hand and aimed it at Garlic's face like a small bazooka. He was just about to swing at me, so hot he'd undoubtedly forgotten where he was, when I wiggled the glass and said softly, "I'll carve up your chops like a Salisbury steak, Garlic. Maybe I can catch an eyeball with one swipe. I asked you please, Garlic, remember? But we can waltz around right here in the ballroom if you want to."

His face kept getting redder, but he didn't take a swing at me. He shook his head, squeezed some air out of his throat. "You sonofabitch," he said hoarsely. "I'll kill you, you son — "

Then he broke it off and walked a few yards away. He stopped and stood there, big paws opening and closing spasmodically. He reached up and rubbed his throat.

There hadn't been any noise louder than that of the glass thumping on the carpet, and very little movement, so I figured nobody had noticed. Vera was closest to where I stood, and she was still ignoring me. I looked around, though, to check, and discovered that the little byplay here had been observed after all.

In an arched doorway across the room on my left, maybe ten yards away, a woman stood looking straight at me. She was smiling. Still smiling, she nodded her head slightly, then waved a hand at me. It seemed likely that Mrs. Redstone had made an appearance. She was quite a surprise.

2

So far in this place, the only woman I'd seen who looked female was Vera, but this gal was a tall, white-haired, and damned fine-looking old party. I knew she was getting on toward sixty, but she must have got off somewhere along the way, because from this distance, except for the white hair, she didn't look forty.

She turned in the archway as I walked toward her, and when I got through it, she pulled drapes to close off the room. She said, "I'm sorry it took me so long to find you, Mr. Scott. Cook's drunk — appropriated a magnum of champagne — and I had to help straighten things out." She smiled. "Including the cook. I'm afraid everything's going to taste like champagne tonight. I'm Mrs. Redstone."

I said how-do-you-do, and she asked me, "Did you hurt the gentleman?"

"Yes, ma'am, only he's no gentleman. The bum — uh — " That, I realized, was a hell of a way to talk about one of Mrs. Redstone's guests.

But she said, frowning slightly, "I don't know who he is. Odd. There's usually a stranger or two at these dreadful affairs, but he's such a *strange* stranger." She smiled. "What was the difficulty?"

I told her all I knew, that Garlic had invited me outside for a chat and that I preferred not to go anywhere at all with Garlic. While I explained, I took a better look at her. Her face was somewhat lined, but she was sure a well-preserved gal, with high, prominent cheekbones and bright-blue, young-looking eyes.

She led the way to two leather chairs across the room, and when we were seated she said, "Let me explain why I phoned you, Mr. Scott. I don't know whether you've met my daughter, Vera, or her husband."

"Andon Poupelle?" She nodded and I said, "I met them both, I'm afraid." I explained briefly what had gone on out there and made it clear that I'd done a horrible job of ingratiating myself with her daughter and son-in-law.

Mrs. Redstone laughed. "We'll get along, I believe. I think Andon's an unutterable boor, myself." She paused. "Do you suppose any of the guests know you're a detective?"

"Garlic must. Maybe some others."

"Actually, it's not important to me if they do know; I hoped your identity could be kept secret, but that was for your own benefit. You see, you're the second detective I've hired — if you accept my offer of a job, that is. The first one was murdered."

A lot of light and gladness went out of this conversation. "Was what?"

"Somebody shot him. I phoned the police earlier tonight about it. A Mr. Samson, Captain Samson, talked to me; that's how it happened I phoned you."

She filled me in. She had two children, twenty-two-year-old Sydney and twenty-six-year-old Vera, whom I'd met. Vera had known Andon Poupelle for less than two months; they'd become engaged three weeks before and got married a week later. Mrs. Redstone was afraid that Poupelle wanted Vera only in order to get next to whatever part of fifteen and a half million dollars might trickle down to her. So Mrs. Redstone had hired an investigator named Paul Yates and told him to conduct a thorough investigation of Poupelle's background, habits, life, the works. Yates had made a report shortly before the marriage, and — according to Yates, anyway — Andon Poupelle was Little Lord Fauntleroy after adolescence.

Mrs. Redstone said, "It almost satisfied me, but not completely. I never did try to talk Vera out of marrying the man — it's her life, after all. But I'm more than twice as old as she is, and maybe just a little wiser." She paused. "It's all my money, Mr. Scott. I inherited it. And my husband married me for it."

Her face didn't change expression and she didn't pause at all as she talked, but for a couple of sentences her voice went flat, with practically no inflection. "He spent what he could, finally drank himself to death. That was fifteen years ago. I didn't want anything like that to happen to Vera. I still don't want it to happen. I've been . . . disgustingly wealthy all my life, so accustomed to a great deal of money that I sometimes forget what men will do for it. For a million dollars. Or fifteen million. Sydney and Vera have all the money they need now, but they'll inherit the entire estate when I'm gone. Naturally I'm anxious to know that no — no fortune hunter — Well, you understand." She was silent for a moment; then she said, "Earlier today I came across this in the newspaper."

She picked a clipping from the arm of her chair and handed it to me. It was only about a dozen lines saying that a local detective, Paul Yates, had been found early that morning face-down on Traverse Road, north of Los Angeles. He'd been shot in the chest and been dead about six hours when found.

Mrs. Redstone said, "This probably has nothing whatever to do with me, with my hiring Mr. Yates. But I couldn't get it off my mind all day. It was the same man I'd recently employed, and there was the coincidence of the location, too. When I phoned, the captain told me, essentially, that the police had nothing to go on yet. And he seemed not to have a very good opinion of Mr. Yates. So I began thinking that perhaps Mr. Yates hadn't been quite honest with me in his report."

"It's possible," I said. "I didn't know Yates personally, but I know a little about him. Pretty thorough man, I've heard, but not above making a fast buck. He might have sold you a bill of goods. Maybe, maybe not."

We talked a few more minutes. What Mrs. Redstone wanted me to do was, first, investigate any possibility that Yates might have been killed because of his work for her; and, secondly, do the job she'd hired Yates for in the first place: go over Poupelle like a vacuum cleaner. She was willing to pay, under the circumstances, much more than the job was worth; my retainer alone was a thousand bucks. I took the case — and the thousand.

"Incidentally," she said, "you may as well have Mr. Yates's report. I just can't make myself believe that Andon is quite the jewel described here. There's something about that man."

"There is, indeed. By the way, he said to me, and I quote, that I smelled like cop. Did he know you meant to hire a detective, or that you had hired Yates?"

She shook her head. "No, and I would prefer that no one know you're involved in this. Nobody learned about the other detective from me. The only source, I suppose, would have been Mr. Yates himself. But that doesn't seem likely, does it?"

"Depends. Clients have been sold out before." I glanced through the papers and put them into my coat pocket. We got up and headed for the other room.

Just before I went out she said, "Actually, there is no great hurry about this. After all, they're married now. But please report to me if you learn anything important."

"Will do."

We grinned at each other and I left her there in the doorway.

In the big room, I looked around to see if I could spot Garlic, but he wasn't in sight. The big man who'd been talking to Garlic earlier was still in the same place. Poupelle stood near him and the movie juvenile; all three of them were watching the ex–Miss America, who was tap-dancing. Vera sat alone on the gold divan. None of them looked my way.

I went to the front door and through it and headed down the drive to my car. The Cad was parked almost out in the street behind a long row of other Cadillacs, Buicks, Jaguars, and money sports cars. I reached my buggy, opened the door, and climbed inside. I was putting the key in the ignition when I smelled him. I froze for a moment, then shoved the key in and started the car. I knew Garlic was crouched in the back of my coupé, and if he had a gun he had me cold.

A black Packard was parked about four feet ahead of me. I put the Cad in gear, stepped on the gas, and suddenly let out the clutch, using my foot on the accelerator as leverage to shove myself to the right as the car jumped forward. My Cad slammed into the Packard with a hell of a crash, but my right foot against the floor boards held me braced against the impact and I was twisting around in the seat as Garlic's right hand, full of .45 automatic, plunged forward, followed by Garlic's surprised face.

The engine died. Garlic jerked his head toward me just as I got set. I swung my body around, drove my own right forward, and bounced my fist off his chin. His head snapped to the side and his gun fell to the seat beside me. I grabbed it, swung it up and around like a discus, and caught Garlic with it squarely on the forehead. He slumped clear out of sight.

I gulped a few huge mouthfuls of air, then got out of the car and hauled Garlic onto the drive. I huffed and puffed and blew him onto the lawn, where I dumped him. I meant to slap him awake and find out if this were his idea or somebody else's — but just then light flashed from the front door of Mrs. Redstone's house.

I looked up as three or four men and women stepped outside and peered my way. That had been a hellish crash.

I hesitated a moment as a couple of middle-aged guys started to walk hesitantly toward me. Then I swore, leaped into the Cad, and started it again. I backed up and twisted the wheel. One of the guys yelled, "You! I say there!" I slid the Cad around on gravel and took off.

In the morning I yawned out of bed and staggered around in my usual early A.M. daze until I'd gulped coffee and toyed with toast. Then I sprawled on the front-room couch and planted the phone on my chest. I called L.A. Homicide and spent a few minutes talking to Samson.

After the amenities, I told him that Mrs. Redstone, overwhelmed by his recommendations, had hired me, and asked if there were anything new on the Yates kill. He was rushed this morning, so he filled me in fast, saying a detective named Carlos Renata, whom I knew pretty well, was on the case and might give me more.

"We got a big nothing," Sam growled, undoubtedly around a black cigar. "Motive's a blank. Probably some hoodlum he slapped around. Shot once in the chest; thirty-thirty slug put a leak in his ticker. Died fast, about two A.M., as near as the coroner could fix it. Looks like he got it there, wasn't shot somewhere else and dumped."

"Rifle, huh?" Sam mumbled something that sounded like "Yeah," and I asked, "What does that mean?"

"Christ knows. It means he wasn't shot with a revolver. We got the slug, a silvertip, good enough to match up with the rifle. If we had the rifle."

"Sam, one other thing and I'll let you get back to your crossword puzzle. I need all I can get — and fast — on one Andon Poupelle and a stinker called Garlic."

"Poupelle doesn't ring any bell," he said. "This Garlic's a low type, does odd jobs like putting the arm on delinquent accounts. Mean boy, goes around tearing down spider webs. Drew bits at Folsom and Q. What's with him?"

I sketched in the business with Garlic and said, "He might have wanted to patch his wounded pride. Could be, though, that he was just earning somebody's fee. I've got his gun, anyway. When I get in to see you later, I'll drop it off. Maybe it'll fit some unsolved jobbies you've got down there. Trade you that for anything I can use. Especially who Garlic's been working for lately."

I told him Poupelle was the former Vera Redstone's new husband, and then he put Carlos on the line. Carlos didn't have much of anything yet, but he did supply me with one interesting item of information.

"This Yates hung around the Afrodite off and on, Afro-Cuban place," Carlos said. "Real wild. Or cool, I guess they'd say out there. Man, the music — they got gourds and things that go clank. And the babe! Man, this gal's named Juanita, see? Sings a little and shakes the maracas. Wait'll you see them maracas."

"Carlos, I thought you were on a murder case."

"She's murder. But, hell, I been working like a dog. I was there on business. This Yates, he hung around there a lot. Was there Saturday night, the night he got hit. Last place we've got him pinned down to; next spot was the dirt road — Traverse. But this Juanita didn't know anything else that did me any good. Man, nothing she did did me any good. Wait'll you — "

"Yates hung out at the — what did you call it?"

"Afrodite, downstairs on Sixth. Poor man's Mocambo — birds behind glass, tropical. Jungle atmosphere. Bunch of hard boys hang out there, too, which makes me wonder. Maybe Yates was on a job, huh? And he got somebody piqued at him. You going out there?"

"Maybe. Depends on what I run into."

"You'll go out there. I know you, Shell. You get anything, let me know." He laughed like crazy.

I hung up. I'd finished dressing and was strapping on my gun harness when the phone rang. I grabbed it and said hello.

"Mr. Scott?"

"Yeah."

"This is Miss Redstone. I need some help, right away. Can you come to see me?"

"Well, hi. Sure, I wanted to talk to you this morning anyway. What's the trouble?"

"I'll have to explain when you get here. But somebody's tried twice to kill me. I'm sure of it. You *are* a detective, aren't you?"

"Yeah, but how did you know? And I thought you were mad at me. Last night — "

"Mother told me; she just phoned me. Look, you'll have to hurry. And I only have a minute. Do you know anything about calisthenics?"

"About what?"

"Calisthenics. Exercises, jump up and down. Mother said you were full of muscles, and that you were an ex-Marine. And I thought surely you'd know some exercises."

"Baby, I know lots of exercises. It depends — "

"I've got to run. I'm at Fairview. You know where that is, don't you?"

"Uh . . ."

"You go out Figueroa and swing off at Maple, then turn left when you hit Traverse Road. About half a mile down there's a fence along the road and a wooden sign over the gate. You can't miss it. Can you get here in half an hour?"

"I could, but wait a minute. What do you mean, somebody tried to kill you?"

"They tried to gas me, and they tried to roll a rock on me. I'll have to explain it all when you get here. You will come, won't you?"

Something was buzzing around in my head, but I couldn't figure out what if was. One of the things she'd said had set off a little bell; which thing, though, I couldn't recall. She'd said so many odd things. "I suppose so," I told her. "Incidentally, I repeat, you don't seem to be angry with me this morning."

"Why should I be angry with you, Mr. Scott?"

"I just thought you would be. And I don't get this calisthenics business. What's that got to do with helping you?"

"We can't let anybody know you're a detective. What's your first name? Shell?"

"Yeah. From Sheldon, if that — "

"Good. We'll call you Don. Don Scott. I'll have to introduce you as the health director. So they won't be suspicious. See you here, then. I've got to hurry."

"Yeah. Health director, huh? Don Scott, huh? You know, you don't make a damn bit of sense." But I was talking to myself. She'd hung up.

I put the phone back in the cradle and sat down while I fumbled through my thoughts. That had been a strange conversation, and one of the strangest things was that the gal hadn't sounded much like Vera. Come to think of it, she hadn't sounded much like Vera at all. And then I got what had been buzzing in my skull. She'd said to turn left off Maple at Traverse Road. I got out the clipping Mrs. Redstone had given me. Yeah, Traverse Road was where Paul Yates had got it. Where he'd wound up face-down in the dirt.

I sat another minute, wondering, then got up, stuck my .38 Special in its holster, climbed into my coat, and left the apartment.

The intersection of Maple and Traverse Road was little more than a bump in Maple. I swung right on the rutted, dusty dirt road and drove a quarter of a mile slowly, then parked. From Samson's description, I knew this was about the place where Yates's body had been found, and I got out of the Cad and stood in approximately the same place where Yates had been standing a couple of mornings ago at about two A.M. It gave me a creepy feeling for a moment, but then I concentrated on the countryside. And countryside it was; I was only about five miles from the Civic Center, but it could have been fifty. A split-rail fence bordered the dirt road; beyond it, grass sloped gently uphill to massed trees. It was green and cool, and there wasn't even any smog out there.

I figured Yates must have been standing just about as I was, looking toward those trees. Somebody by the fence or even a couple of hundred yards away might have drawn a bead on him and squeezed the trigger. It seemed like a funny place for a guy to stand at two in the morning. Of course, he wouldn't have known he was going to be shot. But there wasn't anything out here except dust, grass, and trees, and I wondered what Yates had been waiting for. I got that creepy feeling again, a little tightening of my chest muscles. I trotted back to the Cad, climbed in, turned around, and drove back down Traverse Road.

My speedometer showed I'd gone six tenths of a mile beyond the Maple intersection when I saw the sagging gate. A weathered, faded sign arching over it said, "Fairview." I parked next to it, got out, and stood before the gate, but I didn't see anybody. I couldn't get rid of that sensation of tightness, a crawling of hairs on the nape of my neck.

A length of chain was looped a couple of times around the end of the gate and the fence post, an enormous padlock securing it. Beyond the gate a path was worn, faintly yellow in green grass, going straight ahead for ten or fifteen yards and then curving left behind thick shrubbery and trees. Nobody was in sight.

I looked around for a doorbell — a real city boy, that's me. A tarnished cowbell hung on a frayed rope near the chain and padlock, so I grabbed it and gave it a couple of yanks. Sound clanked over the hills. Nothing happened. A minute passed, and then I heard a whisper of noise, like somebody running.

Then, with startling, almost overwhelming suddenness, a naked tomato swished out from the trees and loped around that curve in the path, straight toward me. Yeah, naked, stark staring nude.

Well, you should have heard me. I let out one hell of a noise.

3

She was a little dark-haired doll and nobody I knew, but you can bet it was somebody I wanted to know.

She wasn't in any terrific hurry; nobody was chasing her. Not, I thought dazedly, yet. She ran right up to the gate and stopped. At least she stopped running, but it was quite a spell before she stopped moving completely.

"Hi," she said.

I still had some of that tightness in my chest, but that seemed to be the least of my worries. I said, "Hello there!"

She smiled, and it seemed to me that she smiled all over. "You're Mr. Scott?"

"Yes. Sh — er, Don Scott. You call me Don."

"Fine. We were expecting you."

Wow, I thought. Maybe my reputation had preceded me. If this was what happened when I was expected, I was never going anyplace again without letting people know well in advance. Hell, I'd flood the States with posters: SCOTT IS ON HIS WAY! I said, "Great. Good. I'm . . . We? Who's we?"

"Miss Redstone told me to meet you and let you in." She stuck a huge key into the padlock, unlocked the gate, and swung it open. It was a monstrous key, and she must have been holding it in her hand all the time, but I'd missed it. "Come on in," she said.

I sprang inside like a gazelle. This gal was about five feet tall, in her early twenties, and cute enough to have looked delectable in red wool BVDs. But in all that sunlight, she was sensational. Maybe she was small, but she had more curves than the Long Beach Fun Zone, and she looked like more fun, too.

She smiled at me again, looked me up and down, and said impishly, "My, you're bigger than the last one. You'll do."

"Do?" I said hoarsely. "Do . . . what?"

"You're the new health director, aren't you? The last one got hurt. He's in the hospital."

"What . . . How was he hurt? *Where* was he hurt?"

She blinked. "A rock fell on him. Didn't you know?"

I pulled myself together a little, remembering that phone conversation this morning. "Oh, yes. That rock. Well . . . "

Man, I was really at a loss. I didn't know what I was supposed to do. I did know, though, that what I was preparing to do was almost surely not what I was supposed to do. The little gal fixed that for me. She damn near fixed everything for both of us.

She turned her back to me and locked the gate. I guess that's what she was doing to it. Then she turned to face me again and said, "You go ahead, Mr. Scott. There isn't much time. Just follow the path, and after about a hundred yards you'll see the buildings. On the left, the long low green room is where you change. You can take off your clothes in there, then go to the main building. It's brown. You can't miss it."

"OK, thanks. Incidentally, I don't think I caught your name."

She smiled again. She smiled a lot. But, then, I had been smiling quite a lot myself. "I'm Peggy."

"Swell. Hope I . . . see you again soon, Peggy."

"Of course. We'll get together later."

I let out another sound, much softer than the first one, but of the same species, then I whirled around and started running up the path, trying to remember where she'd said to go. Most of what she'd said had been just words; listening to her had been like watching TV with the sound off. She'd said to go to some kind of green room up yonder and . . . *No!*

I spun around and raced back to the gate. "Let me out!" I shouted.

Peggy stood a few yards away, eyeing me curiously. "What?"

"I've been stabbed," I said.

"Are you hurt?"

"No, woman. I mean there's been — is — some confusion. What do you *mean* by telling me to go up there and take off my clothes?"

She laughed. "Don't be silly. You didn't expect to keep them on, did you?"
"Lady. Miss. Peggy. Are there people up there?"
"Certainly. About a hundred. All the permanent members of Fairview."
"Come on, tell me the truth. Don't they have their clothes on?"
"Of course not. How silly!"
"Where am I?" I cried. "What is this place? What have I got into? Are you . . . nudists?"
She winced slightly. "Nobody calls us nudists. We're naturists. Health culturists. Sunbathers. Stop pulling my leg, Mr. Scott. Surely you — "
"Level with me now. You're *nudists.*"
She shook her head, then laughed slightly. "Well, I suppose in a sense you could call us nudists, if you must have it that way."
"Well," I said, "I have to go. Really I do. It's been fun, but I really do — "
She was frowning. "Mr. Scott, are you serious? I thought you were joking."
I let go of the padlock and said, "What's the matter? I'm not irreplaceable, you know. But neither am I expendable. So — "
Her face was all twisted up. She acted like a babe about to break into tears. "You *are* serious," she said. "Oh, how terrible! You know we can't get anybody else. Everything will be ruined. The Convention's just day after tomorrow and everybody's worked so awfully hard. You've *got* to help out. It'll break their hearts. Oh-h . . . "
"Hey, relax, honey. You — " I broke it off. This little gal seemed to think I knew a hell of a lot more about what was happening here in Fairview than I actually did know. Maybe it wasn't so smart to show my ignorance so obviously. I said, "I'm sorry, Peggy. It's just that I have a previous . . . engagement."
Her face stayed twisted up for a while, then it smoothed and she glared at me. "You're not going to do it. Most of us have planned a whole year for this. Now you stand right there, Mr. Scott, while I go get Miss Redstone. She'll straighten you out."
She whirled and ran off up the path, arms flying, legs pumping, really in a hurry. I let out a big sigh and fumbled in my pants for cigarettes, lit one, and dragged deeply while I tried to calm down and think logically. It didn't work. Perhaps it was just as well. No matter how calm and logical I'd got myself, what happened next would have sent me straight back to wild and goofy.
Peggy came flying into sight again and cried, "Oh, good, he's still there!" Then she stopped and stood just off the path, panting hard, and I could hear more feet pattering behind her. And then it happened.
Another naked woman happened.
But simply to say "another naked woman" is like saying Mount Everest is higher than some hills. Again it was a woman I'd never seen — and it sure as

hell wasn't Vera Redstone — but I knew this one wasn't getting away from me. Nor was I considering getting away from her. I even took a couple of steps forward as she ran up and stopped in front of me.

She was maybe five-six, with hair like copper and brass melted together by the sun, with eyes a bright, clear blue, with long dark lashes sweeping up from smooth lids. She was deeply bronzed by the sun, and from her tiny waist and flat stomach clean lines swept up to big firm breasts and curved down around sleek, generous hips. She was the picture of health and beauty and sex and sheer joy of living all wrapped up in a completely appropriate frame.

She said softly to me, "Don't say anything." Then she turned her head, the fine lustrous hair flashing in the sunlight, and said, "Go back, Peggy. Mr. Scott and I will follow you."

Peggy nodded, trotted out of sight.

The girl said, "You almost ruined everything, Mr. Scott. Peggy's all mixed up."

I found my voice. "She can't be as mixed up as I am."

"I'm sorry. I guess it's my fault, really. I was in such a rush when I phoned you, and I'm so worried, too. About . . . well, when somebody's trying to kill you, you're not always as intelligible as you should be."

"Miss," I said, "you're not Miss Redstone. I mean Vera. When she — you phoned, I just assumed it was Mrs. Poupelle. That was the only Miss Redstone I ever heard of."

"Vera's my sister. I'm Laurel Redstone."

"Then who the hell is Sydney?"

She laughed. "I'm Sydney. You must have got that from Mother. My full name's Sydney Laurel Redstone. Ever since high school I've been called Laurel — by everybody except Mother. We'll have to hurry now, Mr. Scott, I shouldn't have been gone this long."

Her laugh had been bubbling, merry, full-throated. And her voice was just right out here in the trees and fresh air, like a breath of fresh air itself, soft and warm and a little husky. She was standing about two feet from me, looking up at me with a half-smile on her full red lips. I could see her resemblance to Mrs. Redstone. The strong, high cheekbones and big eyes, the eyes that same soft but startling liquid blue. About twenty-two, Mrs. Redstone had said.

"Come on, Mr. Scott," she said.

"Call me Shell." There seemed little point in being formal.

She turned and walked away from me. I was transfixed, rooted to the ground like an oak. She went about five steps, then turned half around and said softly, "We *must* hurry. The Council is expecting you, Shell." Her smile when she said "Shell" was brighter than the summer sunshine. She kept smiling. Beautifully. And when she started walking again, I was right behind her.

We made the turn into the path and walked silently into the coolness of the trees, branches arching overhead and filtering the bright sun. Well in among the trees I stopped.

"Hey," I said. "I've got to get something straight. Ah, cleared up. That girl — Peggy — told me to, ha-ha, take off my clothes."

She stopped and looked at me curiously. Then she frowned. "Shell, surely you knew what Fairview was, didn't you? When I talked to you on the phone."

"No," I said in a small voice.

"Oh, dear. I assumed that surely you knew. And when you said you'd come here, I . . . " She chuckled. "You must have been surprised." Her features got merrier and she started to laugh. She bent over a little and laughter bubbled out between her curving lips. She laughed alone. But she had a big ball all by herself, then she straightened up and took a deep breath.

I was looking squarely at her, and from now on she could get me to do almost any fool thing simply by taking a couple of deep breaths. She said, "Well, you can't back out now." She sobered suddenly. "If you can't help me, if somebody can't help me, I'm afraid I won't live long. There isn't time to tell you all of it now. But if you'll stay, I'll tell you as much as I can first. Before you decide anything. All right?"

"Does it have to be here?"

"Yes."

I took just as deep a breath as she had taken. "All right."

As we walked up the path, I asked Laurel how she had happened to phone me. She said, "Mother often calls me here, and she did this morning. Naturally I asked her how the dinner had gone last night. She mentioned your being there."

"She say that she asked me to be there?"

"Something about your working for her." She looked at me. "Why would she want a detective? Mother didn't enlarge on her reasons."

I don't know why I didn't tell her but I just said, "Little job is all."

"Well, anyway, I knew *I* needed a detective. Somebody who might help me, at least. I could hardly have a whole flock of policemen running around here at Fairview. Anyway, the important thing is that nobody, absolutely nobody, is to know you're a detective. It must be somebody in camp who's trying to kill me, and if anyone were to find out you're not really what you say — well, it could be awful."

"I, uh, haven't really said I'm anything yet."

"Just bluff it through when you meet the Council. I'm sure you can do it. If they pass you, then you'll be accepted immediately and nobody will guess you're a detective."

"What's this Council? What do you mean, if they *pass* me?"

She didn't answer, because at that moment we came out of the trees and into a large clearing containing three big frame buildings. The biggest building was centrally located, a small swimming pool beside it, beyond that a volleyball court. A little to the right was a squat brown structure, and a long low building was farther over on our left, only about twenty yards away.

Trees ringed the clearing, but in the near distance I could see bodies. Cavorting bodies. The sight shook me. By God, I *was* in a nudist camp. Laurel took my hand and pulled me after her toward the green building. Inside there was a small central room, doors opening into wings on either end. She pointed. "The men's section is there, Shell. Go in and change. And please hurry."

"Uh-huh. Change into what?"

She chuckled again. "Oh, stop it. Go in and take off your clothes."

"I . . . can't."

"Now, hurry. You'll ruin everything."

"But — well, it's just that I'm not a nudist. Never have been. I don't mind nudity. Not in reasonable amounts. But this — this is preposterous!"

She grabbed my hand again and pulled me to the door and pushed me through. "There's nothing to it," she said. "Lots of people do it. It's not as if you were the only one. Look at me."

"Have you noticed me looking at the leaves or something?"

"Anyway, it isn't for long. You'll get used to it." She slammed the door behind me.

I stood stock-still for almost a minute, then said to myself, "Scott, you're being silly. Nothing to it. Everybody does it. Everybody should spend at least one day in a nudist camp, get a new perspective. Hell, you might *like* it," and so on, rationalizing. While I undressed and hung my clothes in an empty locker, I also kept telling myself that though all this wasn't clear yet, at least Laurel was Mrs. Redstone's daughter — one of the two heirs to fifteen and a half million bucks. Maybe what seemed to be happening here had some connection with the case I was already on. It was my duty to investigate. That was it: This was my duty.

In another minute I cracked the door and looked out at Laurel. She was sitting on a small couch, as lovely a sight as I ever did see. She glanced up as the door opened a bit.

"Yoo-hoo," I said. "Well, I did it."

"Fine. Come on out."

"Well, uh, there's something I wanted to ask you. This is something of a strain for me. I'm a detective, you know. I . . . feel uncomfortable without my gun. And this — "

"You can't go wandering around with nothing on but your gun. You'd look silly."

"Can't I, uh, just wear my holster?"

"You can't wear *anything*. Be sensible. It's like going swimming in cold water. Plunge right in and the shock is over in a second."

"OK," I said, and plunged right in. I swung the door wide and stepped into the room.

"Oh," Laurel said. "Come over here and sit down by me. We'll talk a little. I'll tell you about the Council, then we'll go over there."

I sat down beside her, which didn't help my state of mind. She started talking while I examined the woodwork for termites. Didn't see a single termite.

Laurel said, "So it shouldn't take long. Then we'll find someplace where I can explain the rest leisurely. I hope you can convince them that you're really a physical instructor." She smirked. "You're certainly physical enough."

We got up and left the green building, walked to the biggest building, and went inside. She led me down a hall and stopped before a plain wooden door. "In we go," Laurel said.

"What's in there?"

"I just told you. Didn't you hear a thing I said?"

"Not much."

She sighed. "The Council is in there. They're waiting for us. I told you, they have to look you over, size you up."

"They *what*?"

"Quiet. They have to determine if you can handle the job, if you can conduct the calisthenics and games and so on. Darn, I just told you all about it. We can't waste any more time. Get in there."

I put my hand on the knob. Then I said. "It's people in there, huh? How many?"

"Ten. Twelve with us. Six men and six women. Hurry."

I realized that the sight of Laurel Redstone back there at the gate must have swept my sanity away. And the sight of her again in the green room had kept sanity from returning. But I shrugged, turned the knob, and pushed the door open, trying to be casual about it all. I started to put my other hand into my pocket — and the sheer horror of this finally hit me. But the door was open; it was too late.

Laurel whispered suddenly, "Oh, dear. I hope none of the Council members recognizes you."

I whispered back weakly, "Nobody could possibly recognize me. I'm disguised." Then, half-fainting, I walked inside.

4

I got a brief glimpse of an open window in the far wall, a green filing cabinet, a desk with a phone on it, and a floor lamp in the corner in the seconds before I settled on the ten people seated at a long rectangular table on our left. As Laurel and I entered, all ten sprang to their feet. They were, I thought, carrying manners too far.

Laurel guided me, her hand cool on my elbow, to a wooden chair at the near end of the table. In a daze I heard her introduce me as "Mr. Don Scott," then there was a slight rustling as everybody sat down again. I sat down as fast as anybody.

Laurel was saying, "I must apologize for the delay; it was my fault. I gave Mr. Scott poor directions, and since he isn't familiar with this area . . . " and so on. While she talked I looked over the gathering, and this was a gathering a man could really look over.

I'll say this much for the bunch of them: They looked healthy as hell. Probably not one of them had so much as touched a slice of white bread in years. A couple of the gals appeared to be little over twenty; the men ranged from about twenty-five to somewhere around fifty. Laurel and I sat at the narrow end of the long table, four men were on the right side, four women on the left, and at the far end of the table, facing this way, were another man and woman, who were the oldest cats here.

Three of the gals on my left were very nice-looking and the other was satisfactory, but the old babe at the far end was a fit under control. She alone was standing, saying something or other to me, and she looked like one of Fairview's founding fathers.

She was tall, lank, bony, even muscular, and she had a figure like something you might see in a fun-house mirror — straight up and down, with a face like a brown turnip.

" . . . and so," she was saying, "we welcome you to Fairview, Mr. Scott." There was a murmur of assent around the table.

"Thank you, thank you all," I said.

She sat down, then the old guy next to her popped up and spoke briefly. He was built along the same lines as his sidekick, but on him it looked OK. His name seemed to be Frank Blore and he was saying, " . . . so you can understand our dilemma. With our health director in the hospital and the convention only two days away, this is an exceedingly difficult situation. There are, of course, a number of well-qualified men, but unfortunately few of them are naturists." He paused, smiling a little. "So we're certainly inclined to give you the benefit of every doubt." He went on to say how hard all of them had worked to make the convention a success. Nobody had explained to me yet what the hell this upcoming convention was — apparently I was supposed to know already — but even so, I was getting a creepy feeling about it.

Mr. Blore concluded by saying that other members of the Council would brief me on the situation. Then he sat down, and up popped one of the gals on my left, a beautiful, busty, brown-eyed cutie. I stared at the bridge of her nose while she talked, but it didn't help much. She talked for about a minute, then a guy on my right sprang healthily to his feet and boomed at me in a muscular voice.

It was becoming evident that whenever one of these characters addressed the rest of the Council, he or she leaped to his or her feet and plopped down again when finished. I couldn't help imagining the sight they would present in a heated argument.

Somehow or other I learned that the position of health director was exactly what the name implied. He was supposed to direct the "health-building" activities at Fairview: conduct morning calisthenics — before breakfast; supervise games; act as judge in contests; be an authority on nutrition. Their pressing need at the moment was for a man who could quickly take over all the functions of the ex-director, now in the hospital, primarily supervision of day-after-tomorrow's convention. There were going to be people from all over the United States here, apparently, engaging in games, contests, even cooking competitions, and the responsibility for seeing that everything went smoothly rested on the health director's shoulders, since the rest of the Council members all had their own duties.

The talk ricocheted around the table, then the old girl at the end — Mrs. Blore — popped to her feet and said, "What have you to say, Mr. Scott?" and popped down again.

Everybody looked at me. Eleven pairs of eyes focused on me. Then twelve pairs: I was looking at me, too.

"Nothing," I said.

The silence grew uncomfortable. Finally Mrs. Blore got to her feet, more slowly this time, and said haltingly, "Why . . . don't you have any . . . suggestions or recommendations, Mr. Scott? And we're all tremendously interested in your background. Miss Redstone assured us — "

Laurel stood up and said, "Mr. Scott isn't a very talkative man, Mrs. Blore. He's a . . . man of action He was with the Laguna Beach group for over a year, and you'll recall they swept most of the prizes at the '54 convention in San Bernardino." She seemed to be struggling for words and I noticed her hands, white on the table edge, gripping it tightly. She went on, "Before that he was with the Floridans." She stopped, paused a moment as if unable to think of anything more, then sat down.

As Mrs. Blore started to say something again, Laurel turned her head slightly toward me, put one hand over her mouth, and whispered, "Please. Please."

Mrs. Blore said, "It's too late for us to find another person who could help us. We'll give you every . . . " The words trailed off and she sat down. I looked around the table at eleven very long faces, sober faces. Laurel's face looked a little pale under her deep tan. Up till now I'd been in a kind of near agony, primarily concerned with how I could gracefully — or even ungracefully — get out of here. But no matter what my personal feelings were about all this, at least ten people here were seriously concerned about their problem and the success of this convention, which they seemed to have been planning for several months. Maybe I thought it was all a little goofy, but they didn't. And then again there was Laurel to consider.

I still didn't get up, but I said, "Well, it's true I'm not, uh, especially talkative, as Miss Redstone said. But I assumed that you'd all been informed of my background in . . . this work. I don't see any great difficulties. None that we can't work out." Faces brightened all around the table.

Mr. Blore said, "We've really only the sketchiest information about you, Mr. Scott. If you'd be so good as to tell us just a little more . . . "

"Of course. Miss Redstone explained about the Laguna Beach activities. Fine group, that. Never worked with a finer group." I laughed gently. "Until now, perhaps, that is." Everybody laughed gently. I remembered that the first lovely who'd popped up after Mrs. Blore had said something about food preparation and weekly menus, so I looked at her. "Naturally I'll expect you to show me around the kitchen. I'm especially interested in your organic garden."

I didn't even know what an organic garden was; it could hardly be the garden it sounded like. But she'd dwelt on it at some length, so I threw it in. She smiled happily and said: "I'd love to show you around. And of course any suggestions you make we'll give very serious consideration." She had a gorgeous smile.

I said, "One year when I was with the, ah, Sunskinners, we had a food supervisor who came up with a novel idea. He insisted that we peel all our fruits and vegetables, every one. And then eat them. That is, eat only the peelings."

The smile went away. A couple of people said, "No!"

I was losing ground again. "Of course, I put a stop to that," I said, and gained back the ground I'd lost. "I assumed you were all familiar with the fact that I spent several years with the Marine Corps. I've a rather extensive background in unarmed defense, judo, some of the oriental arts of bodybuilding and defense. Oh, yes, everything from yoga to yogurt." I beamed at them.

Mrs. Blore's face lit up like a Christmas tree. "Judo!" she cried. "That would be perfect for us!"

A gal on my left said, "How divine!"

I'd gone too far again. One of the men on my right, a British-type blighter with hair clipped even shorter than mine, said, "Yes, Mr. Scott. We'd all be intensely interested in learning a spot of judo. This is jolly! Could you show us a bit now?"

There were several cries of assent. "Well," I said, "it's not exactly — "

Laurel leaned toward me and looked up into my face. "I'd forgotten this talent of yours, Mr. Scott," she said. "Our last director didn't know anything like it. This *would* do it."

And how it would do it, I thought. Laurel went on, "Can't we have just a short demonstration?"

I forgot myself for a moment and said, "Not with you, babe."

Next to her the brown-eyed busty beauty leaned close and said, "Oh, show me, show me."

I began to get panicky — and then inspiration blossomed. I turned to look across the length of the table squarely at Mrs. Blore. "Why, certainly," I said. "Mrs. Blore, would you be good enough — "

She didn't even let me finish. "I will. Yes, I will." She sprang up and away from the table like a starving ballet dancer. "What do I do?" she cooed.

I slid my chair back and fixed my gaze on Mrs. Blore's chops. Then I took a deep breath and got up and walked over to her. "I'll just run through a few of the elementary items. First, a couple of come-alongs."

"What?" she said.

"Holds. To keep your assailant — I mean attacker — I mean the other party — helpless while you walk him out of the room, or something." I paused. "Should have a pile of blankets — you know, something soft to fall on. That is to say . . . "

Laurel got up, saying she'd go get some bedding, and I looked at her as she hurried out, then quickly looked back at Mrs. Blore. I demonstrated a simple two-finger come-along, grasping two fingers of her right hand in my left, twisting her palm up and lifting. Mrs. Blore went "Eek" softly and up on her toes as Laurel returned.

I said to Mrs. Blore, "Tell me if it gets painful. Easy to break bones this way."

I let go of her hand and she shook it awhile, but looked pleased. Then I quickly demonstrated a couple of the sensitive points on the body — on the upper body — the subclavian nerve pinch and the axillary nerve pinch, pressing in turn the nerve at the base of her neck over the collarbone and the exposed nerve underneath her armpit. Then I said, "Just one more and we'll be through. I'll show you how to throw people across the room."

"Can — can you throw me across the room gently?"

"Oh, I won't throw you far. I'll just throw you down on the blankets." I had to chuckle at the sheer insanity of my throwing *her* down on any blankets. But I was in a veritable frenzy of exhibitionism now, and I said, "Just relax. Here we go."

She was facing me, so I gripped her upper left arm in my left hand and stepped closer, pivoting around so that my back was to her. I wrapped my other arm under and around her right arm; then I pulled on her arm as I bent forward, rolling her over my back and shoulder onto the blankets, graceful as a swan. As she went *kerplop*, I held on in the hope of letting her down easy, but it must have jarred her nonetheless. She waggled her head a bit, stuck out her tongue, and said, "Gah." Then she tottered to her feet.

By George, though, she was a game old gal. "Show me again," she said. This time she got her feet partly under her and cushioned the impact. There was very little else except feet with which to cushion her impact. Then she sprang up and said to me, "You do that so easily. Could a woman do it?"

"Of course. It's not so much strength as balance, timing. You use the other person's strength."

"Well," she said. "You're so strong I should be able to do it easily."

I shook my head. One of us was dizzy. But she persisted, so I showed her just where and how and we made a couple of playful passes at it. Then she said, "I'll try it now." She sounded sort of grim.

I said, "Fine. Ah, easy, remember."

She went into action like a tiger, spun around, slapped her hip into place, and bent forward, tearing at my arm. Just to please her, I gave a little kick with my feet, to help her along — and off into space I went. Mrs. Blore had bent her knees and then straightened up with a snap, grunting a grunt that was nothing compared with what I let out. I spun around in the air like a windmill, and when I landed it was not on those blankets. I landed on a hard floor and I could hear everything rattling around inside me and several internal organs bumped together near my spine with soft squishing sounds, and my head rolled back and went *kerplunk* on the floor. For a little while I just lay there, and I must have been quite a sight, but then everything settled into place and I clambered to my feet.

"That was a *dandy* one, Mrs. Blore!" I squeaked.

She clapped her hands and a lot of noise bubbled around the table. Everybody was beaming happily — except Laurel. She wasn't only beaming; she was damn near hysterical.

I went back and sat down. "Yeah, funny," I hissed at her.

There was some more talk, and finally Mr. Blore said to me, "Now, would you wait outside in the hall, Mr. Scott? We'll reach a decision shortly."

I gave Laurel a hard look, got up, and strode out, trying not to limp. I leaned against the wall for about a minute. Four women strolled by, then two couples, then six or seven more women. I didn't count them, but never in my life had I seen so many naked broads all at once. I didn't mind, though; I'm broad-minded.

Slowly the suspicion was growing: There was a new day dawning in this here nudist camp.

5

People kept wandering by, and it was something of a shock that I realized I might become quite attached to Fairview.

The door of the Council Room opened and Laurel stepped out. This was the first time I'd really looked at her since peeking out of the undressing room, and she seemed even lovelier and shapelier and more everything than before.

She stepped close to me and said in that soft, warm voice, her bright-blue eyes on mine, "Well, Mr. Scott, you are now officially the new health director of Fairview." She smiled a luscious smile. "What do you think of that?"

"I am appalled." I was. "Laurel," I said, "you and I — we've got me into a hell of a fix. And you have some fast explaining to do."

She nodded. "Let's go someplace where nobody will overhear us. Someplace where we can be alone."

"I'm for that."

She smiled winningly — which doesn't mean that I was losing — and said, "I thought you would be. The vote, by the way, was unanimous. You made quite a hit with Mrs. Blore."

"I think I can do without that. Look, Laurel, you must know I can't stick around here. I've got a lot of other things to do."

"I know." She looked around us quickly. "Don't talk about it now. Wait till we get out to the pool."

"Pool? We going swimming?"

"No, and it's not a swimming pool. It's a little lake, a few hundred yards from here. We call it the pool. It's quiet there, and we can be sure we're alone. Come on."

Outside, the grounds were almost deserted. "Where's everybody?" I asked. "There was a sort of parade past me back there."

"It's lunchtime. Are you hungry?"

"No, I couldn't eat a thing. Thanks, though. Let's get out to the pool."

We walked across the grounds, in among the trees, and followed a narrow path that came out into a small clearing. There was a tiny trickle of water at our feet, running downhill, but following its course upward I saw that it came from a narrow cleft between two steeply sloping hills. We walked that way, between the steep hills and maybe a hundred feet into the little valley, actually a sort of blind canyon, and then Laurel stopped and pointed. "There's the pool. Nice, isn't it?"

It was. Fifty yards ahead was the steep face of a cliff, slanting farther toward us at the top than at the base, and the waters of a small lake, about fifty feet wide and three times that long, along the cliff's base. Its surface was flat and unrippled, sunlight bouncing off it. All around the water, but especially at its edge, deep green grass grew profusely. A couple of big white boulders rested on the grass.

I said, "Very nice. Where does the water come from?"

"Oh, there must be an underground spring, feeding it from under the cliff or somewhere. It's usually bigger, from the rains, but it's been so warm this year that it's shrunk a bit. It's a nice little lake, though. One reason the camp was located here."

We walked close to the water, Laurel ahead of me. A knoll of grass-covered earth near the pool rose a few feet above the surrounding ground and Laurel went up it, sprawled at its top. I went up, too, but not as far as she did.

"Sit down, Shell," she said. "We can drop the 'don' out here."

She was leaning back on her elbows, the leg nearest me drawn up with her foot almost buried in the grass, and I thought about walking right past her and down into the water. But I sat down anyway, maybe ten feet away.

"What are you doing way off there?" she said.

"I'll soon be leaving this nu — Fairview. Going to town. And I want to hear what you've got to say. I want complete control of my eardrums. See?"

She smiled. But she didn't say anything right away, so I looked around some more. Anybody within shouting distance of us would have stood out like a bare thumb or worse. We were up in the air a bit, and the ground below our knoll slanted down rather sharply from here. I could see straight out through the niche in the hills a good two hundred yards or so to where the trees started again below us. Seemed rather exposed on this knoll, but maybe it was just my outfit.

Laurel told me about the two attempts on her life. She'd been at Fairview, off and on as the saying goes, for about a year, and almost steadily for three months now. Last night she'd gone to bed in one of the small cabins everybody used here and during the night she'd been awakened by a noise, got up, and found the gas jet of the small heater turned wide open and both windows closed. Earlier the day before, during the afternoon, she'd been with the previous health director, a guy named Elder, when he'd shouted at her, then jumped and pushed her out of the way of a huge boulder plunging down at her from the hillside above. He'd been clobbered by the thing himself.

Laurel, assuming with some logic that somebody was trying to kill her — though she hadn't the faintest idea why — had capitalized on Fairview's sudden need for a new health director to smuggle in a detective.

"Laurel, honey," I said, "I'm going to be plenty busy outside of Fairview. I can prowl around here a little, but that's all. Incidentally, do you know anything about a guy named Paul Yates?"

"Never heard the name."

"Surely you've heard of Andon Poupelle."

"Of course. He's my sister's husband. Why do you ask about him?"

"Just curious. What do you know about the guy?"

"I met him at Mother's about two months ago. He made a big play for me right from the start."

"Not for Vera?"

"Not then. I couldn't stand the man and he finally figured it out. Right after that he started turning his charms on my sister. And she found them more charming than I did, I guess."

"Quite a bit more. She married the guy. Pretty fast courtship, wasn't it?"

"Oh, he's fast enough. He . . . Shell, do you *have* to sit clear over there? I feel as if I'm shouting. Come here."

"Well. Well, OK." I squirmed over to her like a GI sneaking up on the enemy's lines, and I guess I got a little hypnotized. When I was about two feet from this lovely, sensational tomato, and squirming like mad, she said, "Whoa. That's close enough. I don't want to shout, but I didn't mean we were going to sit here whispering into each other's ears."

I stopped, blinked, shook my head, and said, "Wow!"

"Where were we?" she asked.

"Well, I was back there about ten feet, and you — "

"Oh, Shell. I mean, what were we talking about?"

"You mean you've forgotten, too?"

She chuckled. "We were talking about Andon."

"That slob. Yeah. Well, what else do you know about him? Where'd he come from? What was he doing at your mother's place when you met him? Who invited the guy? Wow!"

"I don't know who invited him. There was a big dinner and he was just there. I'd never seen him before. I still don't know much about him. He's something of a gambler, though, I've heard — not professionally, just likes to gamble. I haven't even seen him since that first time, except for the wedding."

"Incidentally, what were you doing at the dinner? Was that before you . . . well, before you came here?"

"No, I've been a member of the Fairview group for over a year. I just signed out and went to the dinner. Mother asked me to come. I hadn't been home in quite a while, so I went." She smiled. "We're not prisoners here, you know. All of us in Fairview are here because we like it, that's all. We can leave if we want to. Some just come out on weekends. I went to Vera and Andon's wedding, but I haven't been out since. It's much more pleasant here."

By this time I was sitting up, sort of leaning all over my knees, and Laurel — still only a couple of feet away, mind you — was half sitting, half propping herself on her hands, which were buried in the grass behind her. I looked up at the cliff beyond her, then back in the opposite direction, out between the V in the hills on either side of us. Something flashed, glinted down near the trees a couple of hundred yards away. I squinted, but I didn't see the flash again, or anything else. Laurel was still talking, saying once more that if the Council ever learned I was a detective I'd be booted out unceremoniously, convention or no convention.

I looked back at Laurel. "Speaking of which, just what comes off at this convention?" I grinned. "I mean — "

She laughed. "I know what you mean. There'll be about four hundred naturists from all over the United States here. Each year the convention's in a different locality; this year it's Fairview. The site was chosen at last year's convention, in San Bernardino, and the Council — all of us, for that matter — have been preparing for it for months. There'll be games, contests, and of course the beauty contest to choose this year's queen."

"Beauty contest? That sounds jolly. Queen of what?"

"Queen of all the sunbathers. You're supposed to be one of the judges, of course."

"Of course. You win."

"Win what?"

"The contest. I vote for you. This judge is fixed."

"I can't compete. I'm last year's queen. So you'll have to vote for somebody else."

"Heck, I name you last year's, this year's, and next year's queen."

She smiled. "Better wait until you see the others."

"I don't need to wait. I have seen . . . enough."

Laurel shook her head. "You're a strange detective, I must say."

"Yeah. Shell Scott, the public eye. Oh, well . . . " Laurel leaned back flat on the grass, fingers laced behind her neck. "Laurel," I said, "don't you think . . . What I mean is . . . "

She turned her face toward me, lips slightly parted. I scooted even closer and said, "Maybe we should be getting back. I've got to get out of here, and . . . it's getting late."

Softly she said, "It isn't late."

"It's later than you think."

The parted lips curved into a soft smile. I looked at her for a second or two, steeling myself, but she was like a magnet, so it did no good to steel myself. I leaned toward those ripe red lips — and something whipped past my head. It snapped by viciously, but I kept on leaning. I almost made it, and Laurel didn't move, didn't look away. Then I heard the crack of sound from far behind me. It was a gunshot.

I jerked my head up as clots of dirt fell from a spot high on the cliff and splashed into the water. Then I let myself fall forward against Laurel, grabbed her, and rolled. She let out a yelp, but I held onto her as we scrambled off the knoll. I grabbed her hand and dived for one of the big boulders, half dragging her with me.

We made it and Laurel said breathlessly, "What happened?"

"Somebody took a shot at us, that's what happened. Stay here." I sprinted toward the sloping hillside, then turned left and ran back toward the spot from which the shot had come. Laurel called after me, but I kept going. Whoever had tossed that bullet up here would have been down below us, in line with the entrance to the pool, and probably in among those trees I'd seen earlier. Right at this moment I'd be hidden from him — if he were still there — but there was a lot of empty space between me and those trees.

When I could see around the hill to the trees again, I flopped onto my stomach and peered down toward them, but nothing moved. Nothing that I could see. For a couple minutes I lay there, staring until my eyes watered; then I got up and ran, bent over, toward the spot where I'd seen that glint of light. I knew that whoever had taken that shot at us must be long gone, but my flesh crawled anyway, and after fifteen or twenty strides I flopped onto my stomach again.

Then I got up and ran clear to the trees and in among them. There wasn't anybody in sight, but by walking a few feet to my right I could see uphill into the V, see the small raised spot where Laurel and I had been sitting, even part of the rock Laurel was behind. At least, I guessed she was still behind it. I knew the guy must have fired from someplace near where I stood; farther back there'd have been too many trees in the way for him to get a clear shot.

He obviously wasn't nearby at the moment. Traverse Road was only another hundred yards or so away, and I tore over there, leaned on the fence, and looked left and right. If a car had gone over that dusty road in the last five or ten minutes, there'd still have been a cloud of dust visible above it; but the air was clear. Nobody'd hightailed it down the road. Not in a car, anyway.

I prowled around a little longer, thinking about cartridge cases, but not really expecting to find anything. Then at an opening in the trees I looked east, and for a moment I thought I was seeing things.

Several miles away was what looked like one of King Arthur's castles. I blinked at it, almost expecting it to go away. But it stayed there, the closest thing to a medieval castle that I'd ever seen outside of those knight-happy movies. I gave it a final blink, then trotted back up toward the little lake and Laurel.

She got up from behind the boulder and walked toward me as I got close. Her face was drawn, sober. "Did you see anyone?" she asked.

"No."

She bit deeply into her lower lip. "This about settles it, doesn't it?" she said slowly. "This was no accident. You've got to help me, Shell. Someone just tried to kill me again."

I didn't say anything. The little grass-covered knoll we'd been sitting on was a few feet to my right. I walked to it, sat where I'd been before, then looked down to the spot in the trees where I'd been, then in the opposite direction, up at the cliff. I could still see the spot where the slug had drilled into the clayey earth, near a patch of clinging green growth. A line drawn from the trees below uphill to that spot high on the cliff's surface wouldn't have met any obstruction on the way — except my head.

Laurel had been lying on the grass. From the spot where I'd been minutes ago, she'd have been barely visible, if visible at all. But my white hair would have stood out like a blond bull's-eye. And, though I liked my thoughts not at all, I started wondering a little about Laurel Redstone.

If I hadn't leaned toward her just before the shot was fired, it would sure as hell have killed me.

6

"What are you doing?" Laurel asked me.

I walked over to her again. "Just trying to put a couple of things together," I said. "The guy had all the time in the world to get lost. He probably hightailed it away right after that one shot."

"Shell, I'm scared."

"That makes sense. I'm starting to get a little jittery myself." I looked at Laurel, thinking again that for everything she'd told me, I had only her unsupported word; even for the item that she was Mrs. Redstone's daughter, come to think of it.

"What are you looking at?" Laurel asked me.

I'd turned from her and was peering up at the cliff face. "Looking at the place where the bullet dug into the dirt up there," I said. "I'd like to get my hands on that slug."

She followed my gaze. "You'd be looking for a needle in a haystack, wouldn't you?"

"I saw where it hit. The only problem is how to get up there."

It looked impossible. There wasn't any place to put a ladder except in the pool, which was no help, and the slug was about sixty feet above its surface. Even a rope let down from the cliff's top, a hundred feet or more higher, wouldn't have worked, because the cliff's top jutted out so much farther than the place where the bullet had dug in.

I said, "Might as well forget it. The only way I could get up there would be to float up, which is a talent I haven't developed yet." I looked at Laurel and said, "How come you chose that knoll — " I pointed to where we'd been sitting — "for our conversation?"

She looked puzzled. "It's pretty, and we'd know there wasn't anybody listening. And there's such a nice view. Why do you ask?"

"We had a nice view, all right. So did that egg with the rifle."

She frowned. "I'm sure you don't mean what that sounded as if you meant. So I must not understand you."

I dropped it. "We'd better get back to camp. I've got to get out of here, anyway."

"You mean you're leaving? After this?"

"That's right." We started walking.

Laurel didn't have much to say on the way back. Halfway to the buildings I said, more to break the silence than anything else, "Laurel, when I was down there in the trees I saw something funny. A kind of castle east of here. Was I in shock?"

"Maybe. But there is a castle out there about four or five miles. Castle Norman."

"A Norman castle? That's pretty silly."

"It's a night club. Drinks, gambling, dinners, floor shows. Owned by a man named Ed Norman. That's where the name comes from." She seemed a little cool.

Now I remembered hearing something about the place. I'd never been there in the months since it had opened, but I'd picked up a few reports about the "delightfully unique" new club. I didn't think any more about it. We walked back the way we'd come, through the trees and then into the big clearing where the camp was. Only now there was an appalling amount of activity.

"Lunch must be over," Laurel said idly.

"It must be digested." Even from here, at the clearing's edge, I could see splashing in the swimming pool and a dozen or so people playing volleyball. In fact, there seemed to be almost every game except leapfrog. And that slightly amusing thought combined with another that had been in my mind. I'd been wondering about that shot at me, and if I might have been lured out here, so to speak, so that somebody could have a try at knocking me off. It seemed like a screwy place for any kill attempt.

But from another angle maybe it was a damned good place for a killing, especially if I were the guy killed. If headlines had blared, "Shell Scott Shot in Nudist Camp," L.A. and Hollywood would have laughed themselves into helplessness. There'd have been more attention paid to *who* got killed and *where* it had happened than the actual fact of my being bumped, and much of whatever investigation was made would have been obscured by waves of wild laughter.

Maybe. It also occurred to me that the same reasoning could apply to Laurel Redstone. There was also the possibility that I was goofy.

Laurel struck out across the open area toward the main building. I caught up with her.

"Where you going? I've got to get my clothes — and my gun."

"You ought to at least sign in. Even if you sign right out again."

"Everybody in camp on records here?"

She nodded. "All the names are in the records, plus the dates of entry. There are photos — portraits — of all of us, too. You can understand why we're careful about who joins the group. The Council wouldn't want to get any curiosity seekers, insincere guests, voyeurs, and so on."

She was still aloof, so I grinned at her and said, "I forgot to tell you. I'm a voyeur. Just a crazy, mixoscopiaed kid."

"Did you want to look at the records?"

"I'd like to."

"They're in the Council Room." We walked toward it.

There were about a hundred people at Fairview now, half of them male, and there seemed a chance that one of the fifty might well be my boy. There was at least a possibility I might learn something from their names and faces. I felt very queer indeed, walking across that bare area so bare myself, but everybody else was obviously in the same fix and nobody pointed or anything.

The Council Room was empty. Laurel went to the green filing cabinet, pulled out a manila folder, and handed it to me.

Inside it was a sheaf of papers and photos. I spread them on the big table, sat down, and went through them. On the left of each sheet was a list of names reading down, next to them addresses consisting only of a city or town name, and lastly the date of admission to Fairview. Another set of papers, one for each day of the month, showed signatures of those who had signed in or out of camp during that day.

Laurel, looking over my shoulder, said, "The daily lists are mainly routine, to show who's here, how many to cook for, and so on. Mainly for the benefit of the cooks. And the health director."

"Yeah." She was not only looking over my shoulder, but sort of brushing against it, and it was disturbing. I concentrated on the pictures and papers.

They didn't tell me much except that there were a hell of a lot of Browns and Smiths at Fairview.

This was July first. Laurel had me sign the sheet for this date, with the time of my entry, and underneath it I signed "Out" and the time, one-thirty P.M. In the month of June only three couples were listed as entering camp: A Mr. and Mrs. Brown on June third, another Mr. and Mrs. Brown on June 15, and a couple of individualists named Waltzinki on June 29. Most of the names had been entered in May.

I mentioned that to Laurel and she said, "Camp really opens May first. May through September is the season. We get a few new guests each month. Of course, some of us belong all year round, come out on the nice days, stay in town the rest of the time."

I looked over all the names but found only what I'd expected; none of them was familiar to me. The pix were no help, either. Laurel put the stuff back and we went together to what I thought of now as the undressing room. In the men's wing I climbed into my clothes, checking my gun to make sure it was as I'd left it. Then I walked back into the main room. Laurel was sitting on the same couch where she'd sat earlier.

"Shell," she said, "can't you stay? What if . . . You know what I mean."

"Yeah. I can't stay, though. I told you that before."

The only thing I knew for sure was that somebody had tried to kill *me* here; and I wanted out of Fairview until I was able to get at least half an idea why. I didn't think I'd find out here. I hadn't recognized any of the photos or names, and I couldn't see asking fifty nudists if they'd taken a shot at me.

The kill try hadn't been for Laurel, and there was a chance she was in no danger at all. Even if somebody had tried to kill her before, it didn't seem likely he'd try again today. Besides, there was no help for it; I had another job to do. I wanted to talk with the old health director. And I wanted to talk with Mrs. Redstone about her daughter Sydney.

Laurel said, "Will you be back?"

She was sitting on the couch, legs crossed, hands clasped in her lap, clear blue eyes fixed on me. Well, I thought, a man has to sleep someplace; I could spend the night here just as well as in my apartment.

"I suppose so," I said.

She stood up.

"Hell, yes," I said. "What made you think I wouldn't be back?"

Her lips twisted into a smile. A small smile, but the first I'd seen for about half an hour. "I wish I could figure you out," she said.

"This previous health director — name was Elder, wasn't it? Where's he now?"

"Palmer Hospital in Pasadena." She frowned slightly. "Shell, why did you ask me my reason for taking you to the pool? Sitting on that knoll, I mean."

I played it light. "Why, I thought maybe I was a better target up there." I grinned at her. "What else?"

It didn't go over with a bang. No smile, no frown even. Just soft blue eyes staring at me, sober and maybe even a little sad. "I'll walk with you to the gate," she said.

"You'd better stick here. With crowds, I mean."

"I'll walk with you. Besides, I have to show you the cabin where you'll sleep if you come back."

"If you don't sit down, I won't leave."

She turned and went out. I followed her. Outside the building she turned right, walked around the corner and a few yards toward the nearby trees, then stopped and pointed. "The little white house there," she said. "See it?"

"Uh-huh. That mine?"

"It's mine. Yours is just beyond it, another fifteen yards or so. I arranged for you to be close to my cabin. In case . . . of trouble," she said.

Laurel had picked up a key to the main gate, which she gave me; then we walked silently to the exit. She told me there was a parking area a little farther down the road and pointed it out. I went through the gate and turned to her.

"I'll see you later."

"Sure," she said.

"Maybe I can find out something about our friend in there." I nodded back toward camp.

"Wouldn't this be the best place to find out?"

"Maybe. Only I don't think so. This is a real funny deal. There are a couple of things I want to check." I paused. "You don't remember hearing anything at all about a detective named Paul Yates?"

She shook her head. "Is he the reason you're leaving?"

"Partly."

"What's the other part?"

I grinned. "You sound as if you were the detective." After a few seconds of silence she said, "'Bye, Shell."

"So long, Laurel."

She turned and walked up the path, disappeared among the trees. I watched her go, waited a few minutes longer, then started the car. I drove on down Traverse Road, yellow dust streaming behind the Cad, then turned on Maple and headed back to town.

There wasn't really a good reason to doubt anything Laurel had told me, I supposed. She'd sounded sincere and honest, and had even seemed a little hurt at a couple of my remarks. One thing was certain: I sure as hell wanted to believe her.

7

Andon Poupelle and his bride were staying at the Gorgon, a high-priced apartment hotel on Sunset between Hollywood and Beverly Hills. A couple of blocks from there I pulled into a filling station, and while the car was being gassed and checked I used the pay phone to call Mrs. Redstone. She answered and I told her it was Shell Scott.

"Oh, hello," she said brightly. "I'm glad you called, Mr. Scott. Have you learned anything?"

"Frankly, I'm not sure. I wanted to ask you about this Sydney you mentioned last night."

"Sydney? What do you want to know about her?"

"I wanted, for one thing, to be sure it was a her. Last night I thought you were talking about a man."

"No. Sydney's my daughter."

"Sydney Laurel Redstone."

"Why, yes. How did you know?"

"I met her."

"Not at Fairview!"

"Yes. You knew she was there?"

"Of course. I even talked to her this morning on the phone. As a matter of fact, I mentioned employing you."

"I wondered about that a little. Lau — Miss Redstone hadn't heard of Paul Yates."

"I never told anybody, even her, about him. Um." She paused. "You can understand that I don't talk about where Sydney is. Not that I mind."

"Sure. How about Vera and her husband? I suppose they know she's at Fairview?"

"Vera does, of course. Andon might, if Vera has told him, I'm not sure." She paused. "How in the world did you learn Sydney was there? I didn't think another soul knew."

I didn't tell her how I'd learned, but asked her to describe Sydney. Her Sydney and my Laurel — I rather liked the sound of "my Laurel" — were obviously one and the same girl. After answering Mrs. Redstone's queries about the odd events of last night, the bashed Packard and the unconscious Garlic, and saying I'd pay for the damage, I hung up. I hung up after Mrs. Redstone told me to forget about paying for the damage.

Vera Poupelle answered the door. A clerk had phoned up from the sumptuous lobby of the Gorgon and I'd been allowed to intrude my beastly presence. Vera had looked very good last night, and she still looked good, but after a view of her sister, especially as I had viewed her, Vera was just another babe wearing clothes. She had on a gray silk dress with a deeply plunging neckline, but so what? I had just been among the deeply plunging necks, and for a while at least I was spoiled.

Her short blonde hair looked as if it had just been fixed by somebody expensive named Pierre or Artibelle, and her lips were smoothly curved, a surprisingly vivid red against the whiteness of her skin. Vera was the indoor type.

"Hello there," I said.

"What do you want?"

"Just a friendly visit. Couple of questions. OK if I come in?"

"I suppose so, Mr. Scott."

She wasn't delirious with joy, but it seemed she was over her mad. She led me to a low divan about eighteen feet long and settled near me.

I said, "How did you know my name was Scott? I don't think I mentioned it last night."

She smiled slowly. "Some fellow on the hotel phone just told me. I thought you were a detective."

I winced. "Sometimes I wonder. Now I'm afraid to ask how you knew I was a detective. Same fellow tell you?"

"Andon did. Last night. Were you the one who assaulted that big, smelly man?"

"I rendered him unconscious, if that's what you mean. Only he assaulted me. He's not a friend of yours, is he?"

"I never saw him before. And I hope I never see him again." She wrinkled her nose.

This Vera was a cute kid, actually. When I'd first seen her in the doorway, her skin had seemed awfully pale, and I like tanned skin and lots of it. But after a couple of minutes Vera's skin seemed more creamy white than pallid. I'm fickle.

I said, "Andon say anything else about me besides the fact that I'm a detective?"

"No. But he wasn't highly complimentary." She paused. "Since you are a detective, what are you doing here? And why were you at Mother's last night?"

I made up a little story for her. "It has to do with that guy named Garlic. I'd like to know where he is. I've been sniffing all over, but he's either far away or not breathing."

"Well, I certainly wouldn't know anything about him."

"I should hope not. Andon around?"

"He'll be here any minute."

I asked her, casually, how long she'd known the guy, and she told me of meeting him at her mother's house, and so on. It checked with the info and dates I'd got from Laurel. Every time she mentioned Andon's name she lit up like a Coleman lantern, and I got slightly tired of hearing her say what a wonderful creature he was. It seemed she was in love with the slob, so I kept my questions reasonably gentle.

"You didn't know him before last May, then?" She shook her head. "Where'd he come from? He an L.A. man?"

"No, he's from New York. He was in stocks and bonds and things there."

"Do you know Paul Yates?"

"Yates? No. Who is he?"

"Fellow I know. Thought he might be a mutual acquaintance of Andon's and mine. Your husband ever mention the name?"

"No."

"You have a sister, don't you?"

"Yes, Laurel. Why?"

"Where is she now?"

Vera didn't answer, narrowed her eyes slightly. "I don't think that's any of your business, Mr. Scott. I don't see that any of this is your business."

"Probably not. I simply wondered if you knew where she was. I already know."

Her eyes widened, then she pursed her lips. "You mean, out there?" She pointed toward the ocean.

I laughed. "No." I pointed in the opposite direction, smack at Fairview. "Out there."

"Fairview," she said. I nodded and she said, "How did you find that out?"

"Is it a secret? By the way, does Andon know she's at Fairview?"

"I should hope not. I mean, I don't think so."

"You haven't told him, then?"

"Don't be ridiculous. I think it's . . . disgusting."

"What's disgusting?"

"Why, they — they run around naked."

"Some of the nicest people I know run around naked. That's what's nice about them. And they aren't even at Fairview."

She was not amused. "Mr. Scott, did you come here to make remarks in such very poor taste, or did you want to see me about something else? I don't care to discuss . . . nakedness."

I said, "Actually I wanted to see your husband about another matter."

You'd have thought he'd been gandering us through the keyhole. The door flew open and banged against the wall and Poupelle came charging in.

"Get out of here, you bastard!" he yelled.

I got up. "I came here to see you."

"I've got nothing to say to you, sluefoot. Now, screw."

I had a feeling this was not at all the way a "stocks and bonds and things" man would have expressed himself. I shrugged and walked toward the door. He followed me outside, as I'd thought maybe he would.

He pulled the door closed with another bang and said, "Mister, don't ever come here again."

"Bag your head a minute. You seemed kind of chummy last night with Garlic and another big boy. Maybe you'll be kind enough to — "

He broke in, his face a brilliant red. "I'll be kind enough to kick your butt down the stairs."

"Poopy, one of these days you'll push me too far, and your pretty teeth'll be few and far between." His flush subsided somewhat. I said, "Anything you can tell me about why Garlic jumped me at the Redstone place?"

He swallowed. "I've got no idea. I told you to screw."

I chewed on my lip a second. "Tell me, just for fun. What's A.T. and T. quoted at nowadays?"

He swung around, went into his suite, and slammed the door again. The neighbors were going to start complaining if he didn't quit that. I went down to the Cad. An uncooperative boy, Poupelle. But he'd told me a little. So had Vera.

It took me almost an hour to get out to Pasadena, visit the Palmer Hospital, and talk for two minutes with a bandaged Mr. Elder, then get back into L.A. Elder didn't tell me anything new, but it checked right down the line with what Laurel had told me. He'd just seen the rock and jumped at Laurel, shoved her, and bang. That was all he knew.

My office is in downtown L.A., between Third and Fourth on Broadway, second floor of the Hamilton Building. I went there and peeked at the guppy tank on top of the bookcase. The colorful little fish had a fit while I dropped some salmon meal into the feeding ring; then I climbed behind my desk and got busy on the phone.

It took half an hour to put out a dozen lines among informants, hoodlums, bootblacks, barbers, bartenders. I wanted information about Paul Yates, Andon Poupelle, Garlic, and any of his chums; any rumbles about people named Redstone, for that matter. And I was willing to pay for it. Much of what I was doing the police had already done, and done better; a number of my own informants, though, would never talk to a cop, but would to me. I might get something. Then I went carefully over the Yates report on Poupelle, the one Mrs. Redstone had given me. There were a couple of items where Yates had been specific enough with places and dates so that I could check his statements. I phoned Western Union and sent a couple of telegrams on those items, added another wire to a detective agency in New York, then left the office.

I started walking, headed for the back rooms, the smelly bars, the dumps and the dives. Some of the boys I wanted to see were seldom near a phone; some of them were seldom sober enough to use one. I'd been over this route dozens of times before, and always it made me a little sick, even a little sad. Lower Main Street and Spring, Los Angeles Street, the whole area I tramped, has a kind of horror about it in the daytime. At night the softer lights and shadows hide some of its squalor, but in sunlight it's hard and ugly.

I saw white-bearded men sprawled in doorways, wrapped in the sweet smell of wine; a young, empty-eyed man sitting on wooden steps at a dingy hotel entrance, his fly unzipped, something crusted on his chin and shirt front. I talked to an amazingly thin middle-aged woman with bones showing everywhere and a face like a skull with skin stretched over it, her voice mumbling as she stared at me fixedly from dark, burning eyes. But I didn't get a single slice of useful information. It's funny, but among the derelicts and hoodlums and alcoholics around me, there were probably the answers to a thousand crimes. There's an "underworld wireless" that they all seem to have an ear on. Often a torpedo can get knocked off at noon in Miami and the whispers will be going around among the stumblebums and small-time hoods in L.A. before the sun goes down. So I kept walking, talking, buying beers, and spending quarters. For two bits a man can buy a bottle of port. But I didn't get anything solid until almost four-thirty P. M. And even then I wasn't sure.

About that time a small-time grifter named Iggy the Wig, a bald-headed hoodlum who wore a rug to keep him glamorous, caught up with me in Jerry's, a beer joint on Main. He was one of the guys I'd phoned earlier. We sat at the bar and I bought two beers and gave one to him.

Iggy poured down half of his and said, "About Yates. Yeah, I heard a word. Not big, but I know who can tell you. Lemme think a sec." He pulled at his beer. "What's it worth — if I can think of it?"

"A fin."

"A sawbuck?"

"A fin, Iggy. Give, or burp up that free beer."

"Scott, a saw ain't much. This guy, he's gonna want a C. That's what he said."

I almost fell off my stool. "He going to Europe? For that kind of dough he must have pooped Yates himself."

"Nah. OK?"

I nodded.

"Three Eyes," he said. "You know him?"

"Yeah, I know him." He was a middle-aged character with one good eye, one glass one. I never did understand how that made him Three Eyes. He was so spindly and white and frail that he always looked as if he'd just come from donating blood and they'd forgotten to turn him off. He'd been in the money on several occasions, sometimes in the big dough, but he always wound up with empty pockets and an empty bottle.

I said, "Hangs out around Third and Main, doesn't he?"

"Not any more, he don't. He's scared about somep'n. Got hisself a room. I know where I can get him, bring him here. For a double saw."

"What's he scared about?"

"I dunno. Not for sure. There's a rumble about that Poupelle, too, and some kind of push. Three Eyes was runnin' off at the mouth about it. Maybe he can tell you. He must have somep'n. Deal?"

I sighed. This Iggy was a grifter, all right. He started out asking for five bucks, got a hunch I might pay a hundred to Three Eyes, and tapped me for twenty. "All right. Get with it." I gave him two tens and he slid off the stool.

"Take a while," he said. "I gotta go there. How about cab fare?"

"Get going, Iggy."

"Make it here, OK? Say six."

"Six."

He left. I finished my beer, thinking. The Afrodite was only three blocks away, so I started walking again. I tried to recall the girl's name, the entertainer Carlos had mentioned. I needn't have bothered. It was plastered all over the outside of the club: JUANITA. Juanita with the Cubaneros. Juanita singing, dancing, entertaining. Everything but pictures of her.

The Afrodite was a cellar club on Sixth, down a short flight of cement steps to a pair of thick wooden doors. The doors were locked, so I pounded on one of them. I could hear a mumble of voices inside, but nobody let me in.

I kicked the door a couple of times. The voices stopped, footsteps thumped toward me, and I heard a bolt slide back inside. A white-jacketed man, the bartender, I supposed, cracked one of the doors and squinted out at me. "Yeah?"

"Place open?"

"Nah." He shut the door on my shoe, looked down. "The foot," he said. "Move the foot."

"I want to talk to you a minute, friend."

"The foot. Move — "

He was cut off by a deep voice from inside. "What's the trouble, Joe?"

"Some big ape got his foot stuck in the door. Wants to talk or something."

The deep voice said, "Ask him who it is."

"Who is it?" Joe said. "I mean, what's your name?"

"Shell Scott."

He relayed the info. There was near silence, broken by undistinguishable conversation for almost a minute. Then: "Let him in, Joe."

8

Joe shook his head, then stepped back and opened the door wide. "You heard the man," he said.

I was getting a funny feeling about the Afrodite. I hadn't ever been inside the place, and already I was less than crazy about it. But I walked in. There was practically no light, or so it seemed until my eyes got accustomed to the change from the brightness out on Sixth. Then I almost wished it were darker. I'd walked in on two of the toughest hoods in town — the two I recognized; and the other two men with them looked at least as ugly. There was a woman there too; I'd seen her around with some of the racket boys. All five of them sat at a table close by on my left.

The guy with the deep voice said, "Be damned if it isn't Scott. What an honor for all us fellows."

He was Chinese, a young, completely bald guy in his early twenties, maybe two inches taller and twenty pounds heavier than I. He'd been a star center in college, and once, while he'd been carrying a big rally sign that said "Football," the sign had got torn and he'd run around carrying the part that said "Foo." He'd carried that name into his postcollege and extralegal activities, and because he was a youthful Chinese egg and bald, and because hoods are hoods, his moniker had become, almost inevitably, Young Egg Foo.

Foo had played center on that team so long that something had happened to his brain. Besides which, he had become suspicious of everybody. And he had no sense of humor, no graciousness. Ask him what time it was and he'd hit you over the head with the clock. That kind of guy.

With him at the table was a lop-eared gunman named Strikes. I remembered the gal as an ex-queen of the burlesque circuit. Five years ago she'd been in the big time, right at the top, known as Bebe Le Doux. But now she was Babe Le Toot, and in her set there were lots of gags like "Hey, boys, let's go on a Toot," and "I got a Tootache," and so on. The two other hard-looking men sat on either side of Babe.

"Hi, Foo," I said finally.

There was no reply, no more conversation, so I walked to the bar. In the wall behind me, beyond a pane of thick glass, soft lights illuminated a bunch of fake trees and vines, and a couple of dozen odd-looking tropical birds with brilliant plumage. A small dance floor was a little to my left and behind me as I climbed onto a stool.

The white-jacketed guy went behind the bar and I said, "Got a beer?"

"Place don't open till seven. What you want to talk about?"

Foo said from the table, "Give him a beer, Joe. It's on us, Scott."

I said thanks without turning around.

The bartender opened a bottle of Acme and slid it over the bar. "You don't use a glass, do you?"

"Not here. Tell me, Joe, did you get to know Paul Yates very well when he was hanging around here?"

He was wiping the bar top with a limp rag, and when I said "Paul Yates" he paused for a fraction of a second, then went on wiping. The soft buzz of conversation behind me stopped at the same time.

"Don't think I know the man," Joe said.

"You must know him. I understand he was around here quite a lot. Here last Saturday night. A soft heel."

"Like you?"

"Not quite. He's dead."

The buzz of conversation behind me hummed again. A wall mirror ran left and right behind the bar; in the dimness I could see the five of them. Just so there were five of them.

"Still don't know the man," Joe said.

"Try these. Andon Poupelle." No reaction. "Garlic." He kept on wiping the bar. I said, "Juanita. Ever hear of anybody named Juanita?"

He grinned. "Can't say I have. Don't know anybody you mention. I'm never gonna know anybody you mention, chump."

I took a long pull at the beer, set the empty bottle on the bar, and said, "Joe, I'll bet you don't even know what day this is."

He looked puzzled.

"This is the day you got hurt," I said. "You cracked so wise you threw your whole face out of joint." I grinned at him and looked at my watch. It was almost five P.M. "At five o'clock it happened," I said. "Just a couple of minutes from now. So let me ask you again about Yates."

There was movement in the mirror. While Joe stood there licking his lips as if they had molasses on them, I watched the mirror. There wasn't any sound of chairs being pushed back, but three figures stood up around the table. Behind the glass wall, a couple of birds flapped around. Two of the guys walked toward the bar. The other one went to the front door and stood there with his back, to it.

Young Egg Foo sat down on the stool to my right. The other guy was one of the two I didn't know. He took the stool to my left and slammed a beer can noisily on the bar. He was short, very chunky, wearing a white T-shirt so his big biceps and knotted forearms would show.

Nobody said a word. I eased my stool back a bit from the bar, mainly to see if it would move. It moved. Muscles, on my left, put the beer can between the palms of his thick hands and squeezed it together without apparent strain.

"My name's Kid," he said to me. "Just Kid. Be pleased to meet me. How you like that?" He held the squashed can between two fingers.

"You cheated," I said. "You used both hands."

His upper lip lifted slightly while he rolled that around in his head. But I was paying more attention to the bartender than to Kid. Joe wasn't looking at me, but at Foo, out of sight on my right. When Joe winced a little, I pushed with my hands on the bar, shoved backward, and let my feet hit the floor, then bent down in the same motion and grabbed the bar stool at its base — just as Foo's fist whistled by where my head had been.

That big fist was even bigger because of what looked like two pounds of metal wrapped around his fingers and resting against his palm. If he'd hit me with those knucks he'd probably have split my skull, but he missed and by that time I was coming up swinging the stool.

Foo was forward, pulled off balance by all that weight on his right hand, and he was all spread out when I hit him. But it was nothing to the way he spread out after I hit him. The metal of the stool's top bounced off his bald pate with a heartwarming clunk and he reeled back against the bar, his arms splayed out. Kid grunted and I spun back toward him, straightening my legs under me as I moved.

His fist smashed into my chest and threw me back a step, but I caught my balance as he jumped toward me. I was still holding the stool about head-high, arms stretched to my right, so I drove all four legs at him as hard as I could. One of the legs caught him on his left cheekbone. The metal was covered by a rubber cap, but it got him solidly and snapped his head to the side.

A chair crashed over at the table, but I couldn't look around. Kid was dazed just enough and I wasn't going to let him clear his head at this point. I swung the stool around in a circle and slammed it against his skull. Kid might never again clear his head. He went down like a poleaxed ox.

I started to swing around, but didn't make it. A fist bounced off the side of my neck and somebody crashed into me. I got tangled in the bar stool and went down, the guy on top of me. His hands jabbed at my throat as I rolled away from the bar and across the floor, but he hung on. I got my knees under me, squeezed my hands together, and brought them up hard inside his wrists.

His arms flew apart and I drove my right fist at his gut, knuckles stuck out from my palm, but they hit high on his chest. I didn't knock him out but I sent him sprawling backward. Feet clumped on the floor behind me. I started up, but a shoe caught me in the ribs. Pain sliced up my side.

I got turned around, on my feet, just in time to see Strikes with his right hand drawn back and in it a leather-covered sap. His teeth were bared. I let him swing and ducked aside, the sap grazing my hair. Then I grabbed his arm in both hands, swung my body around, and bent him over my hip.

I bent him hard. I put all I had into it, pain and anger jumping in me, and I threw that bastard over me and six feet through the air. He smashed into the glass wall with a horrible crunch.

The guy on the floor was coming up as I swung my foot at his chin. One of us timed it just right. My shoe jarred into the side of his face and his jaw snapped out like part of a rubber mask. He made a little sighing sound and collapsed. His jaw stayed out, oddly twisted. So did he.

I swung around. Nobody else was coming at me. Hell, there wasn't anybody left except Babe Le Toot.

For a while I didn't know what the shrill squawking sound was. Then I realized it was birds. Birds cackling neurotically and flying out through the busted glass, flapping around the room. A couple of feathers floated gently down to give the room a nice nightmarish touch.

I didn't see Kid, though. I thought I'd addled his brains for him, but he wasn't on the floor. A door in back stood open. Foo was hanging on the bar, halfway up it again. Christ, he was tough. I jumped toward him, but he didn't seem to notice me. The bartender stood rooted to the floor.

"Joe," I said, "give me a bottle of whisky. A full bottle."

He uprooted himself.

I took the bottle by the neck and banged it on Foo's head. He slithered all the way down. "Call the cops, Joe," I said.

There was a sound like gargling over where the birds had been. I walked over and looked inside the shattered glass. Strikes lay on his back, all over blood. His face was red and wet; a big flap of skin hung down from his neck. He was breathing, and I saw little bubbles dance in the redness.

Joe was on the phone, saying something. I walked to the table. Babe still sat there, drinking some kind of green thing.

"Mister, you're in real trouble," she said.

If my neck and side hadn't been hurting so much, I might have laughed like a banshee. "What was it I just had?"

"A little trouble. You've really had it now, you have."

"Maybe. Explain a little more, Babe."

She wasn't explaining anything today. Besides which, she was plastered. She'd just been sitting around with the boys having an afternoon cocktail, she said, and cutting up old touches. They were hard guys, they were, and they had plenty of hard friends, they did. The friends wouldn't like this, she said. I remembered Carlos saying that maybe Yates had got some of the Afrodite clientele "piqued at him." It seemed I'd got them piqued at me now.

I sat where I could watch the bar, Babe on my left. Joe had hung up the phone and was standing quite still, not looking this way. Babe Le Toot was a big girl, about five-eight or nine, and she still had the generous curves that had sometimes got her as much as a thousand clams a week at the New Follies and other bump-and-grind parlors. She wasn't much over twenty-five now, though her face, especially her eyes, looked older.

She was humming. "St. Louis Blues." She was so far into her cups of green stuff that she slid off the tune half the time, but I remembered now it had always been her big number, the climax of her act. I'd seen her once at the New Follies here in L.A. wearing a G-string that only went up to A, slithering around the stage while the pit band played a hot, rasping, gut-tickling "St. Louis Blues." She'd been good, almost bumped the house down. Maybe she was remembering that; she sure wasn't talking to me.

I heard a siren, got up and took another look at Strikes. He was still bleeding, still breathing. Foo wiggled a foot over by the bar, scraping it along the floor. A bird flew past my head. The siren ground to a stop out front and heavy feet slapped down the cement steps. I went to the door, slid the bolt back, and let the boys in.

The first man inside was Nat Hoving, a detective sergeant. As I swung the door open, a cockatoo went by him and outside with a raucous squawk. Nat yanked out his gun and squawked louder than the cockatoo.

Then he recognized me and said, "What in Christ's name is happening, Scott?"

Some more cops pressed in behind him. I gave them the story, then pointed at Strikes. "He needs a Band-Aid," I said. "There was a young one called Kid, too. He must have staggered out back. You know him?"

Nat said, "I know a punk called Kid hangs out at Fleming's Gym. Didn't know he was running with this bunch. Christ, what started this bloody mess?"

"They did, but nobody told me why. I was asking about Paul Yates." Nat nodded. I said, "You know who these bums work for?"

He shook his head. "Mostly self-employed, I'd say. We'll check it downtown. Besides which, we'll ask them."

Ten minutes later a doctor was working over the alley heroes. Joe was swearing he didn't know anything about anything; all he did was serve drinks. The police took everybody downtown, including Babe. I told Nat I'd be in later to check on this with Samson and sign the complaint. Joe locked up as we left, leaving the birds perched practically everywhere. Nobody ever found that cockatoo.

It was six-fifteen when I got back to the beer joint where I was supposed to meet Three Eyes. Iggy wasn't around. I called the bartender over.

"You know Three Eyes?" He nodded. "I was supposed to see him here."

"You Scott?"

"Yeah."

He looked me over. "Back in the head. Nervous type."

I walked to the men's room. It looked empty, but when I said, "Three Eyes?" the door of one of the pews cracked and he looked out at me. His face was thin and bloodless, even paler than usual, I thought. His good eye stared at my face, but the other one aimed at the middle of my chest.

"Christamighty, where you been?" He came out. "You got the money?"

"Yeah. But I don't know if what you've got is worth a C."

"I dunno either, Scott. I got to have it — I want to blow town. Tonight, maybe. Pretty soon, anyway. I got bees in my butt. I need a stake."

"Are you broke?"

He looked sadly at me. "I'm stoned. I'm flatter than them French fashions. I'm so — "

"OK, you're dying. So I'll toss in a ten for nothing. What's got your wind up? Come on out and I'll buy you a shot."

"I don't wanna be seen with you." He paused. "Maybe you don't wanna be seen with me, neither. Just what you after, Scott? Iggy don't make things too clear."

"Paul Yates. Andon Poupelle. Anything about people named Redstone." I went on to include Garlic and the guys who'd jumped me at the Afrodite.

He licked his lips and looked at the floor. He said, "I'm down on my luck right now, but a month or so back I was in OK, had a good roll. I went out to this new place outside of town, this castle, and rolled a few. I seen this Poupelle there, an' he was sweatin' plenty, losin' every time."

"You were at Castle Norman, huh?"

"That's it. Well, Poupelle dropped a hell of a pile. You've seen how they look — he had that green, gone look. Sweat rollin' down him. I was cashin' in a little pile, and I heard him chinning with the boss man, tryin' to pass some paper. He couldn't cover with cash. Anyways, he wrote out a check, played a while more. I seen it, and asked somebody who the guy was — you know, man's got to keep on his toes." He grinned at me. "I left after a while and didn't think no more about it then."

Three Eyes had been screwing up his face, twitching the skin around the glass eye, and now he turned and went to the washbasin. His back was to me, but I saw him dig at the eye, then turn on the water and hold something under it. I lit a cigarette while he kept talking.

"A week or two ago I hear a rumble around among the boys. It goes that Poupelle passed a check for maybe fifty Gs, maybe more, and he's got nickles."

"It bounced, huh?"

"That's what I hear. But he's still walking around, so he must have covered it somehow."

I said slowly, "He's got lots of nickles now, Three Eyes. Any more?"

"Yeah. I go out to the castle a couple times since. He's there, Poupelle is. He wins, he loses mostly, but he plays all the time — and all the time green, like before. Well, that's about all. Any good?" He turned off the water faucet.

"Might be. But not good enough."

I knew he had more, and he'd spill all he had — unless he thought he could get the hundred cheap. Three Eyes was another of the guys you had to drag information out of, and for a hundred bucks I meant to keep dragging. He wouldn't have asked for so much cash unless he was pretty sure I'd fork it over. I'd done business with him before, too; he'd never look at you when he was holding out. That's why he shot craps; he always lost at poker.

"You know a con guy named Bender? Don't know his first handle."

"Can't place him."

"He's local. Ran with McGinty and his boys. Understan', Scott, this is all air. Just a rumble. Nobody pinned it down for me, but the word's all over. Rumble is, Poupelle pushed this Bender."

"Poupelle? He killed the guy?"

"That's the word. It's just air, remember. Supposed to of happened at the castle. That's all, all I got." He still wasn't looking at me.

"OK. It's worth twenty bucks. What else you got?"

"Funny thing. You're the second guy what asked me about Poupelle. I gave him the same tale — about the check, I mean. He seemed to like it."

"When was this, Three Eyes?"

"Last month. Say a couple weeks after I was there at the castle."

"I think I know what you're getting at. Spit it out."

He turned around and looked at me, a trickle of water running down his cheek like a tear. "You guessed it," he said. "It was Yates."

9

I dropped my cigarette on the cement floor, stepped on it. "What else, Three Eyes?"

"That's it. But I read about him. About Yates. And I like everything peaceful. Now gimme the century and I'll blow."

I gave him the money, adding ten bucks to it. He crammed it into his pants pocket, mumbled his thanks, and started to leave. I stopped him, had him narrow the dates down for me as best he could, then let him shuffle off. I followed him outside, watched him walk to the corner and turn; then I went back to the office and picked up the Cad.

Driving down First Street, I thought about what he'd told me. The thing that puzzled me most was the rumble about Poupelle's knocking off this guy Bender. That didn't fit anywhere. I stopped at the Central Station on First and Hill, left the gun I'd taken from Garlic with Kennedy in the Scientific Investigation Division, then drove on to City Hall and went up to Room 42. Homicide.

Samson was in the front office with two of the detectives on the night watch. They were all drinking coffee from paper cups, and there was a chorus of helloes when I came in. Sam tossed off his last swallow and crumpled the cup in a heavy paw. Phil Samson, Homicide captain, is a big, tough career cop with iron-gray hair and a jaw like a battering ram. That jaw is a lot like Sam — big, formidable, and determined.

The jaw was thrust forward now, and his sharp brown eyes were fixed on me. "Hear you ran amok again, Shell."

I found a wooden chair, straddled it, and said, "Somebody did." Sam growled a lot, especially at me, but it was just noise. He was a good man, and a good friend. We'd worked together on various cases ever since I'd opened my office, and that friendship had saved my neck more than once.

"I gave that forty-five of Garlic's to Kennedy in Ballistics," I said. "You come up with anything I asked about this A.M.?"

He shook his head. "Still the same. Haven't tied Garlic in with anybody. Not a thing on Poupelle, not here. We're checking with Sacramento and Washington." He scratched his chin. "Well, what happened at the Afrodite? Tell it here if you want, and I'll get the paper to Masterson."

He called in a stenographer, who took down the story as I ran through it. I signed the statement, shoved the papers across the scarred wooden table, and said, "That's all I know. Might be they just felt playful. It looks like more than that, but I can't tell. Maybe they can."

"Afraid not," he said. "They're sprung."

"Come off it, Sam. What's the gag? They wouldn't be sprung this soon."

"Oh, hell, no," he growled. "Just ten minutes before you got here is all. That Chinese character made his call to his attorney, and then bang. Next thing Judge Curry had issued the writs, even called us up himself and yelled a while. Your pals are out on the streets right now." He grinned wolfishly. "Probably waiting for you, so they can thank you."

I stood up. "Why, you old bastard! Why in hell didn't you tell me this when I walked in?"

"I figured you'd jump out the window. And I wanted your story on paper while you were calm and judicious." He smiled bleakly. "Justice must be done."

"Judge Curry, huh? Why would a superior-court judge be so damned interested? Who put up the surety bond?"

"Rio Bonding Agency on Temple — Mac Rio, you know him." Sam paused. "We had to let the boys go, but Strikes isn't out yet. He's in the hospital jail ward, but he's not talking to anybody. And he'll probably take off soon as he can talk — if he ever can again."

I swore. "Fast work. Maybe those bums are more important than I thought. To somebody." I was quiet a minute. "Sam, I picked up a rumble about a con boy named Bender, local talent. It goes like this: Andon Poupelle hit him in the head."

"He what?"

"Poopy pooped him. Just noise floating around, the man said. It's yours for what it's worth; that's all I know."

Samson got out one of his horrible black cigars, lit it with a wooden match. Between puffs of what looked like green smoke he said, "Bender. That might be Brad Bender. We haven't heard anything about him. That's all you know?"

"Except that it's supposed to have happened at this Castle Norman outside of town." I grinned. "By the way, I hear they gamble out there. I'm thinking of reporting it."

Samson scowled. "You go ahead. Report it to Kefauver. You know Ed Norman, Shell?" I shook my head. "He's a hard boy that stays clean — no matter how dirty he gets. Follow me? He's got more friends than Dale Carnegie. Different type of friends, maybe, but big ones."

"That way, huh? I'm going out to see the man tonight."

"Watch yourself. Don't spit in his eye or anything. I'd hate to lose my job getting you out of some fool jam."

"Come off it. Norman can't have any friends with that kind of pull."

Sam didn't smile. He bit into his cigar and said quietly, "Of course not." After a pause he said, "OK, Shell. We'll check it. And thanks."

I had a quick cup of coffee with them and left. I drove over to Temple Street, stopped and talked a couple of minutes with Mac Rio at his bonding agency. We weren't friends, but we'd done business before, and he did tell me that he'd got a phone call about springing Foo and the boys, and putting up bond. He wouldn't tell me who had called. I headed for Castle Norman.

Remembering my first view of the place from Fairview, I went out Figueroa to Maple, then turned right on Traverse Road, drove past the spot where Paul Yates's body had been found, and kept on for another three and a half miles. Yeah, you could go to Castle Norman by this route, too.

It was almost eight P.M. when I went up over a small hill on Forrest Street and caught sight of the medieval eyesore as I started down. In another minute I was there.

A battery of high-powered floodlights pushed back the darkness, illuminating the club and grounds. Except for the lights, the three or four acres might have been yanked from five hundred years back. Forrest Street, a black asphalt road, curved in from the highway through a lot of green lawn toward the castle. There was a big parking lot on the right of the club, with perhaps thirty cars in it.

The Castle itself was remarkably realistic, complete with towers, crenellated battlements, everything except a jousting tournament. A stone wall several feet high surrounded it, and this side of the wall was a ten-foot-wide ditch filled with muddy water. A moat, yet. There was what seemed to be a drawbridge lowered over the moat, though whether it actually worked or not was a moat question. The final fillip was a character in armor mounted on a white horse that stood under the arched stone entrance at the far end of the drawbridge. The guy held a long staff in his right hand, a colorful cloth dangling from its tip. A final anachronism was the neon sign under the stone arch: "Be Medieval in the Modern Manner."

I parked in the lot next to a low-slung gray Bugatti, got out, and walked toward the drawbridge. As I approached the entrance, the guy in armor kicked his horse in the flanks and started clop-clopping across the wooden drawbridge. What some guys will do for a buck, I was thinking.

Apparently the knight's function was to welcome arriving guests and give them a big thrill. This time, though, something seemed to change the script. The knight swiveled his head toward me, looked straight ahead again, then did a creaking double take and wheeled his nag around to go clattering back over the bridge.

I stopped and looked after him. Whether the guy was somebody I knew or not would be hard to say, because he was well hidden behind his armor, but he could have seen me easily through the slits in his visor, and he'd acted as though he'd recognized me. If he did know me, apparently he didn't want to know me any better.

I walked across the drawbridge. Beyond the wall there was an open space to cross before reaching the actual entrance to the castle, and several tables were scattered around in it, most of them under a huge, heavily branched oak tree. Only half a dozen customers were at the tables, having dinner. The castle towered in the air before me, a pair of big wooden doors straight ahead. Another armored knight, this one without a horse, opened the doors, and I went inside.

Sound bubbled out and washed over me as I went into a big room where about thirty people were sitting and standing, most of them with highballs. A few were eating, and I saw several silver ice buckets keeping bottles of champagne cold. I had a hunch it would cost ten bucks just to get a beer in Castle Norman, and the clientele bore out that assumption. Mainly the guests looked like sugar daddies with their sugars.

A few suits of armor were scattered around the big room. Against the right wall was a bar of highly polished dark wood, and I meandered over to it. I meant to order a drink while sizing the place up, but I didn't have time. I was still trying to catch the bartender's eye when a husky guy in a tuxedo came out through a set of red draperies in the rear wall and walked up to me. I swung around on the stool to face him.

"You're Shell Scott?"

"That's right."

"You're gonna have to leave."

"I just got here, friend. And I'd like to see — "

"Don't gimme no guff. On your way, Scott."

A tough guy. An optimist. I opened my mouth to tell him in one pithy phrase what he could do, but then snapped my jaws shut, counted to ten by fives, and started over. "Simmer down. I came here to see the boss, Ed Norman. How about telling him he's got a visitor?"

He sighed, wrapped a hand around my elbow, and tugged gently. I guess that was supposed to settle everything, but all it did was play hell with several of my glands. I could feel my face getting hot. "Mister," I said quietly, "back up a couple of yards and I'll tell you something."

Husky frowned and said, "Huh?" But he kept looking at me and finally he dropped his hand to his side.

I went on: "I came here to see Norman, and I mean to talk with him, unless he comes out here himself and tells me to blow. You can tell me all night, friend, but the only way you'll take me outside is carrying me piggy-back. And before you carry me, I'll have to be unconscious. So how about telling the boss he's got a visitor?"

Husky grinned at me. "I might carry you out, at that." He glanced around at the crowd and shrugged. "Have it your way."

He spun on his heel, went to the red drapes and through them. I let out some breath and looked at the bartender, who seemed to be purposely ignoring me. It was as if the Castle Norman employees had been told in advance that the big egg with white hair was contagious.

I never did get the damn drink. In a couple of minutes Husky was back. "OK, tough man. Let's go see the boss."

I slid off the stool as he turned and headed back toward the drapes. There was a big door beyond the drapes, and though it was painted to look like wood, when he rapped on it there was the ring of metal. The door opened, and we walked through.

There was noise here, too, but more subdued, mixed with the unmistakable whir of that little ivory ball in its slot on the roulette wheel, the clank of one-armed bandits. Here were the tables Three Eyes had told me about.

On my left were two roulette wheels separated by a dice table; on the other side of the room were two tables for craps and one for roulette. Slot machines lined three walls, and there were also half a dozen twenty-one tables.

Following Husky past one of the dice tables, I saw a blonde head that looked familiar. The nice slim body was in an orange jersey gown this time, but even from the rear it was Vera Poupelle. I got a look at her profile as she swallowed at something in a cocktail glass.

My guide kept trudging ahead as I stopped by Vera. "Hello," I said. "Making millions?"

She turned and let blue eyes roam over my face. "Not making anybody." She smiled. "Mr. Scott," she said. "How nice. And you?"

I grinned at her. "I haven't even started playing."

Her smile faded and I noticed her eyes were a little glassy. "That's right," she said. "I don't like you, I remember."

"Sure you do."

"No. If Andon doesn't like you, then I don't like you."

"Now, why wouldn't Andon like me?"

"Ask him." She pointed with her cocktail glass.

Poopy hadn't even noticed me, he was so intent on the game. Stacks of blue and red chips were lined up in front of him.

"That's enough," a voice said on my right. It was Husky, my guide. "Come on," he said.

"Just as soon as I say hello to my friends."

"You must not of heard me, Mac." He wrapped his fingers around my arm. "Come on."

"Relax, friend. Relax the fingers."

He must not have heard me, either. He yanked and said, "Mr. Norman doesn't like to wait for guys."

I grabbed his fingers and squeezed them a little. The wrong way. He started looking vicious.

I excused myself from Vera and walked around the table. Husky rubbed his fingers a second, then came after me.

I stopped by Poupelle. "Hi." He turned toward me, preoccupied with the play, and I didn't give him a chance to get set. As soon as his eyes fell on me I said quietly, "What ever happened to Brad Bender, Poupelle?"

He gasped and his face was suddenly drained of color. His jaw sagged, and for a moment I thought maybe he was going to faint, but then he recovered slightly, clicked his teeth together, and turned away from me. He fumbled with the chips in front of him, but his hands were shaking and he was toppling stacks all over the "Don't pass" line.

I'd got more with that crack than I'd bargained for. I'd damn near scared his pants off him. And then there were those fingers on me again. Husky yanked me hard, swung me around to face him, and said angrily, "All I got to do is whistle, you bastard, and there'll be ten men here playing games with your head."

Some people you just can't coexist with. Husky's left hand was clutching my right wrist and his other fist was balled, held in front of him. I reached across my body slowly with my free hand, looking at his face, and trying to smile pleasantly, but as soon as my left hand closed around his wrist I stopped smiling.

I jerked my arms up, pulling my elbows in close to my stomach, pushing with my right wrist against his loosened thumb and pressing the thumb of my own hand forward against the back of his hand as it turned. Husky grunted and twisted to his right, mouth coming open as I got both thumbs together on the back of his bent hand and leaned into it. And then he was facing away from me, left arm sticking out behind him, and bending over like a man trying to bite the carpet.

I didn't want him stooped over like that, the center of all eyes, so I stepped close to him, bent his arm up behind his back, then held it with my left hand while I transferred my right hand to his right biceps and straightened him up. He straightened almost eagerly, because I was digging my fingers into the axillary nerve underneath his armpit. Now we could coexist nicely.

He whistled, but so softly that nobody more than three feet away could have heard him, like a tire going flat. I glanced around. The whole operation hadn't taken more than four or five seconds. Two people were looking at us. I put on a big, toothy grin and wiggled my eyebrows at them. The puzzled looks went away and they chuckled. It was nothing after all; just a couple of slobs.

"OK," I said to Husky, "let's go see Norman."

He started to say something, but I put a little pressure on the fingers of both my hands, and wondered idly if the pain going up his left arm would meet the pain going up his right arm. "You just lead the way," I said. "And don't talk about calling guys to play games with my head. I'm in a beastly mood tonight."

We made it, chums together, to the rear of the room and to a door there that I kicked a couple of times, gently. It opened and another apelike stranger looked out and stepped aside. As we went past him he walked along with us and said to my guide, "What's the matter with him? Huh?"

I answered for Husky, who wasn't able to say much of anything. "I can hardly stand up," I said, grinning at him. "He hit me in the stomach."

He grinned back at me, as if that pleased him. Then his grin went away. He looked at Husky. "Why's he so happy about it?"

Then we were at another closed door. The mental giant opened it, let us through, then pulled the door shut behind us, remaining outside. This would be Ed Norman's office, and the big heavy-faced guy behind the desk would be Ed Norman. His coat was still too tight; he was still stolid and unsmiling. I'd seen him before — last night, in fact, at Mrs. Redstone's. The tall, broad character who'd been with Garlic, and briefly with Poupelle. Some wheels started spinning in my head. There were several questions I'd wanted to ask Ed Norman, but now it seemed unlikely that I'd get any answers. None, at least, that I'd like.

10

I said, "So you're Ed Norman."

"That's right, Scott. And . . . What in hell's the matter with you, Foster?"

Foster, no doubt, was the large gent I was so wrapped up in. I'd tightened a little on seeing Ed Norman, and I had consequently tightened Foster. He was bent forward with his mouth wide open, making little noises.

I said, "He got fancy with me. I don't quite know what to do with him now that I've got him."

The muscles at the sides of Norman's thick jaw bulged, then relaxed. Last night I'd noticed his marked-up face, and now I saw that he had a scar at the side of his right eye, another over one cheekbone. They looked like knife scars. Norman said, "You push your luck pretty far, don't you, Scott?" He said it casually, his deep voice soft, almost soothing. It didn't soothe me, though, and I didn't answer.

Norman got up and walked to the door. He opened it and said, "Get out, Foster." He looked at me. I turned Foster around, gave him a shove, and let go of him. He staggered toward the door, but whirled before reaching it and started to move back toward me.

"Out," Norman said.

Foster hesitated, glaring at me, then spun around and stalked from the room. Norman shut the door, then went back behind his desk. He pointed to a chair and I sat down in it. His phone rang.

He picked it up, grunted, and listened, keeping his gaze on me. Then he hung up and sat quietly, staring at me, a big silent hunk of cold-rolled steel bars and springs, with eyes like the eyes of a dead fish. Except for those eyes, he wasn't bad-looking. The scars just made him look more like a guy who might wrestle with the devil. And maybe win.

He blinked, as if he'd been miles away, and suddenly produced a big smile. "Well, Scott. What was it you wanted to see me about?"

Norman was being charming, mine host, but he was not an actor. That smile had all the warmth and friendliness of Nome, Alaska.

I smiled back and side-stepped his question a little. "I didn't realize you were the guy I saw at Mrs. Redstone's last night. With Andon Poupelle and Garlic, I mean."

He frowned slightly, but kept that skull grin in place. "Yeah, I saw you there. But I wasn't with Andon or — what was that other name?"

"Garlic."

"Said hello to Andon, but I was with some other people. Friends of mine. You working, Scott?"

"Uh-huh. You never heard of Garlic, I take it."

"Nope. Who you working for?"

"Client. Odd you never heard of Garlic. He was going to bash my head in last night, or maybe shoot me. I thought maybe you'd sent him at me. Didn't know you were Ed Norman last night."

He chuckled through clenched teeth. "You know now."

"Sure. Speaking of Poupelle, didn't he slip you a stiff a while back? For fifty Gs or so?"

"Well, now. How'd you find out about that, Scott?"

"Got it off the wire somewhere around town. It's the McCoy, huh?"

"That's all settled now."

"He paid off?"

"It's all settled."

I grinned. "That figures. I see Poupelle's still playing little games next door. Must mean he paid up, right?"

"Scott," Norman said, unsmiling now, "you better dig a finger or two in your ears and get all the weeds out of them. Now you tell me something. You didn't come out here just to ask me about Poupelle, did you?"

I didn't know what the hell to tell him was my reason for coming here. I'd expected somebody else, not the guy from last night's party, not someone apparently chummy with Poupelle. And I had the uncomfortable feeling that, despite my asking most of the questions, I'd told Norman more than he'd told me.

But I had to give him something fast, so I said, "No, I've been trying to run down this Garlic creep. He had at me with a forty-five canister, besides which he exhaled at me. So naturally I'd like to chat with him."

"What made you think I could help you?"

"I heard he'd been here a time or two. For a little crap-shooting."

"I told you I never heard of the man."

"True. I didn't know that until I came here, Norman."

"Now you know. So I guess we've got nothing more to talk about."

"Right." I stood up.

Norman said, "Hope you won't take this wrong, Scott, but I'd rather you didn't come out to the castle any more. Matter of fact, I'll have to insist that you don't." He gave me that skull grin again.

He went on to say something else but I wasn't paying attention to his words. There was an upholstered chair in the far corner of the room, beyond Norman's desk. It seemed like an odd place for a chair to be. I looked at its base. The office floor was covered with a beige carpet, and under the chair, but not quite hidden by it, was a darker spot. If somebody were to be shot, I thought — somebody like me, say — and he bled on the carpet, and the blood were then mopped up, the stain would look very much like that darker brown spot.

Norman was saying, " . . . know I don't have to tell you twice, Scott. But I'm glad you got out here this once."

Sure. He was tickled to death. I said, "No, once is enough for me. Nice place you've got here, though, Norman. See you."

I didn't want to leave; I wanted to prowl around this office a little. But I like things neat and tidy, and one spot on the rug here was plenty. This damn place was a fortress, anyway, and in the event that Norman decided he didn't want me to walk out, I'd play hell getting through a couple of steel doors even if I managed to cold-cock the guy. I left.

At the first steel door the large man stood, still wearing an expression that indicated great perplexity. He looked at me for what seemed a long, long time, and I could imagine him thinking. Now, where'd I see dis bo before? Finally he grunted, turned, slid back a bolt, opened the door, and let me pass through without a word.

Poupelle and Vera were no longer in the game room. I looked around for them, then asked the dealer at the dice table where Andon had been playing, "What happened to Poupelle? The guy that was shooting craps here."

"Mr. Poupelle left about five minutes ago. He was ill, I believe, sir."

"You see him leave?"

He nodded.

"Poupelle go straight out? Or did he maybe make a phone call first?" At either side of the room were small stands on each of which was an ivory-white phone.

The dealer blinked. "Why, yes, he did make a call, sir." He pointed across the room at one of the small tables. "I noticed because he seemed so ill."

"He may have thought he was dying. Probably phoning a doctor. Thanks."

I went to the phone, looked up the Afrodite's number in the directory, and dialed. This was an outside line, not a house phone, but a man could still dial Norman's office phone number easily enough. Good old Dr. Norman. He fixes things. I suddenly wanted out of here and far away, but I let the phone buzz until I was convinced the Afrodite was closed before I hung up.

Foster let me through the door, glaring at me, but I felt sure he wouldn't do anything except glare. Not here with all these witnesses. I went out through the front room, where there were more aging Romeos and adolescent Juliets, but no Poupelle. The knight on the drawbridge still sat on his horse.

I kept my eyes busy as I walked to my convertible, then drove slowly out of the parking lot. Once out of sight of the castle, though, I tramped on the accelerator hard for a mile, then swung right on a side road and doused the lights.

In half a minute or less a sleek black car ripped past like a rocket. I lit a cigarette and smoked it, wondering, then put the Cad in gear and headed for Fairview.

With the Afrodite closed, there wasn't a great deal more I could do tonight. Besides, I wanted to sort out in my mind the bits and pieces I'd come up with today and this evening. And there was another reason for going back to Fairview: I wanted to see Laurel again. I wanted, of course, to be sure that she was all right, that there hadn't been any trouble during my absence from camp. But besides all that, I just wanted to *see* her.

I found a parking space in the lot and left the Cad in it, then locked the main gate and walked up the path toward the center of the camp. As I approached the low green building I looked to my left, where Laurel's cabin was dimly visible in the moonlight. There weren't any lights burning inside the little house, and I supposed she was asleep.

It was very quiet as I walked toward the small white cabin. A soft, warm wind blew from the north, rustling through the trees, but that was the only sound other than the crunch of my footsteps. At the left of the door a window was raised, opened wide, frilly curtains billowing inward. I knocked, the rap of my knuckles surprisingly loud. I waited, but there was no sound from inside. A small, cold worry started nagging at me.

I knocked again, then stepped to the window and poked my head inside. "Laurel," I called softly. "Hey, Laurel."

More silence. I tried the door. It was unlocked, and I went inside, felt for the wall switch, and turned on the lights. A door was open in the far wall. That would be Laurel's bedroom, since the cabins had only two rooms. This room was simply furnished with a table, three cushioned chairs, and a small couch. I went into the bedroom, turned on the light.

The bed was mussed but empty, as if Laurel had lain there for a while and then left. I was sweating.

As I turned out the light I noticed a glow through the rear window of the bedroom. I walked to the window and looked out. There were lights in another cabin a few yards behind this one; from what Laurel had told me this afternoon, it was probably my cabin. I turned off the front-room light, went out, and trotted around the cabin to the one where the light was showing.

I didn't even stop to look through the window in front, just twisted open the door and went inside. This cabin was an exact counterpart of the other one, and I hot-footed it across to the bedroom and went in.

She was on the bed. I walked over and looked down at her. The light filtering in from the front room was barely bright enough so that I could see it was Laurel. She lay on her side, but twisted so that her shoulders were almost flat on the bed, the light-blue spread pulled partly across her body. She was breathing deeply in her sleep. I stood over her for a while, letting my own breathing become more normal, oddly surprised to find that all my muscles had been tense, my nerves tight. The roof of my mouth was dry.

In the soft light, her features relaxed in sleep, she looked even lovelier than she had in daylight, and younger, more defenseless. The blue spread covered her hips and thighs, leaving her lower legs bare, and only half covered the full globes of her breasts.

Right then I knew that whether I liked it or not, I was getting involved, emotionally involved, with this lovely. During the afternoon thoughts of her had come into my mind often, but I'd pushed them away, telling myself that she'd be all right, there was no reason really to worry about her. But these last minutes had been bad ones for me; it had frightened me to find her cabin empty, frightened, me more than I cared to admit to myself, and then seeing her had been a relief that was almost a shock. I didn't stop to ask myself why she was here; it was enough that she was safe, warm and alive.

I stared down at her, feeling the tension and tightness drain from me. Then her breathing stopped. I saw her move slightly, convulsively, and her eyes were open wide. She gasped, rolled away from me, and scrambled off the foot of the bed, jumping toward the door.

"Laurel!" I yelled.

She stopped, one hand against the doorframe. "Shell?"

"Yeah, honey. What's the matter?"

Her shoulders sagged a little, then straightened. She turned. "I didn't know it was you. I thought — I was asleep, and . . . " She didn't finish it.

"Relax," I said. "It's only me, the — the confused health director. Remember?"

She laughed softly, nervously, and said, "You startled me, Shell. Let me get hold of myself."

"I'll tell you what, Laurel. You'd better go wrap yourself in the bedspread again, or both of us will get hold of yourself. Or ourselves. I mean, I have just come from the outside world, where everybody — "

She laughed, more naturally and freely this time, and walked away from the door to the bed. She walked right past me, too, within *inches* of me, while I made faint, unintelligible sounds.

"Sit down, Shell," she said. "I'm all right now."

"You bet you're all right." I looked around for a chair. No chair.

"Sit on the bed," she said. "I won't bite you."

I said, "All right for you, then; I won't bite you, either," and sat down on the edge of the bed.

Laurel threw a bit of the bedspread over her. It was just a little bit of the spread, draped with almost studied, and certainly artistic, casualness. Draped far more casually than I.

"Well," I said, "I guess, ah, I'd better get back to my place. Ha-ha. *This* is my place, isn't it? Nice having your place in my place. I mean, *you* in my place. Yes."

"I'm sorry I acted like such a fool, Shell. I woke up and saw you there, only I didn't know it was you." Her voice was soft and warm, as if that wind outside had come sighing into the bedroom. "You see, what startled me so much was that you had your clothes on."

"It was? Well, that's, uh — " I cleared my throat. "We can fix that, all right."

She went on: "That's the last thing you expect to see here in Fairview, a man standing over your bed with his clothes on."

"Yeah. Guess I should have turned the lights on, what? Still can, you know." I sped on. "Shall we get a little light on the subject — in the place — in the house? This chatting away in blackness is for the birds." My voice sounded like an old man's, but I didn't feel very old. I felt full of youth, full of beans, full of wild, red-hot corpuscles that were scorching my brain and everything. "Laurel," I said in a cracked voice, "Laurel, do you remember when we met? I mean, how I explained that I'm all full of beans — ah, that I am not used to — "

She leaned forward and pressed two soft fingers momentarily against my lips. "Don't go on so," she said. "What's the matter with you?"

"Don't you know?" My voice went way up.

67

She chuckled softly, "Yes. Of course I know." She paused. "Shell, I came here because I was . . . frightened. There alone in my cabin, and not knowing when you'd come back. Or even if you would. So I came here and waited and fell asleep. I was afraid to be alone. I feel better now, but I'm still afraid . . . to be alone."

She had risen up on one elbow to press her fingers against my mouth, and now she still held herself partly off the bed. Light from the front room, seeming brighter now, cast a silvery mistiness over her bare shoulders, and over proud breasts that looked smoother than ivory, softer than down.

She was looking at my face, her long-lashed eyes almost closed, lips parted. "You won't be alone," I said. I leaned closer to her and she tilted her head slightly, and I saw the tip of her tongue flick against her lips just before they parted even more. Then they were against my mouth. At first her lips were softer than the whispering wind outside the cabin, but then they writhed and curled against mine, and her tongue flicked against them again as we both moved closer together and our arms went around each other.

Her lips clung to mine for a long time, her hands against my back, fingers curling, then her lips went slack and her head rolled to one side. I kissed her throat, the curve of her shoulder, the soft warmness of her breasts, and she breathed rapidly, making small sounds deep in her throat. Then I felt her move against me; her lips traced my cheek and touched my ear as she whispered to me.

I got up. When I slid into bed beside her again, barely touching her, she was lying motionless on her back. For long seconds she lay that way, unmoving. Then slowly she turned toward me, pressed her lovely soft body deliberately against me.

I said her name once, and once she said mine, but that was all. There were no more words after that. No more words except that, some time later, Laurel said in a thick, sleepy voice, "Night, Shell, darling," and I said to her, "Good night."

11

I woke up suddenly in the morning. I woke up suddenly because Laurel was wallowing all over me, shaking my head and saying, "Get up. Wake up, Shell. It's time to get up."

"Yeah, sure," I said sleepily. "Call me in a couple of hours or so." Here was this beautiful naked babe wallowing about, and I tell her to call me in a couple of hours. I'm just not myself in the morning.

The wench said, laughing, "You've got to get up. You have to lead the membership in calisthenics."

It hit me all of a sudden. I grabbed the covers and threw them away from me, burying Laurel under a sheet and blanket, and sprang clear out into the middle of the room. "What!" I shouted.

There was a flurry of bedclothes and Laurel's tousled hair and beautiful face emerged from them. She was grinning.

"Calisthenics," she said. "You remember." Then she stifled a delicate yawn and stretched, arching her back and thrusting with small, tightly closed fists at the ceiling. The covers slid down. And down.

Now that I was about an eighth awake, this was an entirely different proposition than that earlier wallowing had been. I sprang back onto the bed. "Ah, yes! I remember! Calisthenics!" I grabbed her.

She squirmed briefly, laughing, then slid out of my clutches. "You got away," I said dismally. "I guess I'm still not awake. Not enough. Come on. It was your idea, remember."

"Oh, you're crazy! Look, there are a hundred people you've got to lead in calisthenics."

"Say that again. I never heard of such a — A *hundred?* Hellfire, woman, I didn't even know it was possible with more than one or two. How am I — "

She had scooted off the foot of the bed and now she interrupted me. "Shell. Listen carefully. Every morning before breakfast the health director leads all members of Fairview in calisthenics. It gets the blood circulating, stimulates you, wakes you up, gives you an appetite."

"Not me, it doesn't."

"It's for health. Tones the body and blood, gets oxygen into the lungs. And you're the health director. Pretty soon the bell will ring. There it goes."

She was right. There it went. It sounded like somebody beating on a metal triangle with a sledgehammer, and a horrible sound it was.

"Come on," she cried, and spun around.

"Wait. Where you going?"

"We're going to the front of the Council Building. You're supposed to be there already. At the bell, everybody runs out there and lines up. Then you face them and tell them what to do."

"I'll tell them what to do, all right," I grumbled. "But as for facing a hundred crazy — "

"Come on!"

"Wait! Suppose I *should* get out there. What do I do?"

"Calisthenics!" she cried, then sped out the front door.

I ran out after her, but at that point I didn't really intend to lead those nudists in calisthenics, I was just running after Laurel. I honestly didn't know quite where I was yet, and Laurel looked like a rambling aphrodisiac that was rambling away from me. I could see her fairly well, flying ahead there, because the sun was just coming up, casting a cold light over everything. Cold. It was pretty cold. All over me it was cold.

I stopped. "Wait!" I shouted. "I forgot my pants!"

She stopped, too, ran back to me, and grabbed my hand. "I'll not stand for any more of this nonsense. You — "

"Nonsense, fooey. I'm serious. I forgot my — "

"Come along with me. Please, Shell, please, hurry, please."

She was tugging me after her, and when she said please that way, a man would do almost anything. I went along with her, trotting just behind her, and then she let go of my hand and rambled ahead again. I will never know quite how it happened. I only know that I was intent on Laurel's fanny, which was about a yard ahead of me, and then suddenly it was gone. In its place was something I shall not even tell you about, much less describe.

I realized that Laurel and her gorgeous fanny had tricked me. They had lured me out here onto an open plain in front of a hundred naked people. They all looked at me. I looked at them. This went on for an eternity, and during all those years I kept trying, fruitlessly, to think of possible means of escape, ways I could get out of here without anybody being the wiser. I couldn't think of any.

I could see Laurel again now. She was a short distance to my right, in the center of a row of about a dozen people. And seven or eight more rows of people were lined up behind that front row. I backed away from them as the sun seemed to spring up over the horizon as if the fool thing thought it was high noon. When I was maybe twenty feet from the front row I overcame the impulse to wheel and run into the woods and got control of myself.

I was stuck with this. I had to lead these characters in calisthenics; I was the health director, even though there had probably never been a health director who felt more nauseated than I did, and by God I would show them a thing or two. Ha-ha, I thought sadly, as if I haven't.

I plunged into it. "Go-ood morning, everybody," I said. Suddenly my voice was thin and fluting. Everybody chorused, "Good morning." Those hundred voices boomed out over the hills.

"Here we go," I shouted. "Fall out."

Nobody moved. They didn't understand. Hell, that was nothing. I didn't understand, either. "Well, fall in," I said. One guy clear over at the end of the last row, next to the pool, made a splash. There was a titter of laughter.

I couldn't fool around any longer. But then I noticed something strange. All hundred or SQ of them were standing scrunched over in a very damned peculiar position, with one leg lifted, bent at the knee, and held before them in a protectively coy gesture. I thought they had all gone nuts, but then I understood.

I let out a hollow laugh and straightened up. The hell with them. "All right now, men," I shouted. "And women. Let's ah, allez oop. Here we go." I sprang into the air clapping my hands, and I never felt sillier in my life.

Talk about silly — you should have seen those nudists. They went up into the air like small fizzled rockets, and came down bouncing, and then popped into the air again. I was springing up and down like mad, clapping my hands like a 205-pound Nijinsky, and they were trying to keep up with me. I tried to think of something else to do, some other goddamn calisthenic, but it's pretty hard to think of anything sensible when you're leaping about clapping your hands, so I just kept on.

I had, until now, thought I knew something about calisthenics. I had known nothing about calisthenics. I was looking at the world through rose-colored people and I was, as they say, all shook up. Besides which, I was getting pooped.

So I stopped. Everybody stopped.

From there on everything happened in a kind of a daze. I ran in one spot for a while, then I spun about, and then I did numerous other things, and finally some deep knee bends with my hands on my hips, all of which those people did, and it was that last one that finished me. I knew I couldn't go on.

"That's it," I said. "That's all. You're dismissed. *Go away!*"

The gathering broke up. People tottered off in all directions; others just sank to the ground where they were. Tired, huh? I'd sure fixed them. Healthy, hah, some healthy bunch. I began to feel faint.

I sat down on the grass, the landscape reeling. Somebody reeled toward me, then plopped at my feet. It was Laurel. She glared stonily at me, chest heaving, and when that chest heaved, it *heaved*. Finally she gasped, "What happened to you? You trying to kill everybody? Woo. You must have pranced around out there for an hour. Woo. I think everybody's going back to bed. Woo."

"Woo, that's a fine idea. Let's go back to bed. Woo. Get it? We'll — "

"Oh, shut up." Laurel was all out of sorts. "You'd think you were training us for the front lines. All we needed was guns and packs on our backs. You're not still in the Marines, you know."

"I wish I was."

"Well, if you did it on purpose, I hope you're satisfied. But I'm proud of everybody at Fairview. Nobody quit. Nobody fell out. Nobody had a stroke."

"Honey, I didn't do anything on purpose. This is part of some dark fate that pursues me. But, by George, you're right." I thought about it a minute, then looked around. Unbelievable as it was to what was left of me, there was already a game of volleyball in progress. Half a dozen people were splashing in the pool. And I lay here quaking in every limb. Even Laurel's breathing was almost back to normal, and I was snorting like a male ape downwind from Tarzan and Jane. "Hey," I said, "maybe there's something to this health kick after all."

"Of course there is," she said.

"I could sure use a smoke," I said, feeling for one. Naturally I had no goddamn smokes. I was sprawled there on the grass in the sunlight, in just my skin. "Guess I better not smoke, anyway," I said. "Wind's bad enough as it is."

I had thought I was in pretty good condition. But I felt no great pride in that thought at the moment. Of all those people who had been sprawled on the grass, only two besides Laurel and me were left. A man and a woman. Memory came slowly back to me. During a particularly strenuous conniption I had seen one of them reel, stagger about, and then fall like a stone. The other had gone into an almost identical routine shortly afterward. At the time I hadn't thought about it, but now that the frenzy had passed I began to worry about them.

I got up, and it was a long way up; then I walked over to them. They lay as if dead. I poked the man with my toe and he grunted. Then his eyes opened. He said, "You sonofa — "

"Ah, ah," I said. Good, he was half alive. "You all right?" I asked him.

"You sonofa — "

"Hold it, my friend. A lady is present."

He stirred himself. "Fran? Where's — " Then he got his head craned around and lamped her. "You've killed her!" he shouted. "You've killed Fran! You sonofa — "

But then the babe let out a long moan. He patted her face, then looked up at me and grinned, a slim-faced guy with brown hair and lots of teeth showing. "Sorry," he said. His grin went away, then he put it on again. "I'd like to be excused from calisthenics tomorrow morning, dear director." He was either grinning or snarling.

"Sure." I grinned back at him. "You're both excused. All three of us are — "

The gal let out another moan and sat up, wobbling her head. She was a nice-looking babe about twenty-five or so, whose shape appeared to be in better shape than she was. She had long black hair and deep, dark unfocused eyes. "What happened?" she said.

Laurel came up alongside me then and after a few more words the two revived characters got up and walked away. "No casualties after all," I said to Laurel. "They must be new here. Like me."

"Not quite. That's Mr. and Mrs. Brown. They've only been here a few weeks. I think it was mean of you — "

"Hey, get it through your head I was *out* of my head. Brown, huh? Everybody's Brown here."

"There are only four sets of Browns, and I don't like your insinuation. Shell, you don't seem to understand that almost everybody here stays at Fairview because they like the life — and I don't mean that in any smutty or cheap way at all. Bob and Mary are wonderful people, and so are all the rest. It's a healthful way of living here, healthful physically and mentally, and — "

"Whoa, sweetheart. Don't get me wrong. And I believe you. Give me a little time to adjust. Why, I even know some voodoo experts, and yogis, and Democrats, and I like 'most all of them. But I had to get used to them. OK?"

She shook her head. "I suppose."

"Incidentally, who are Bob and Mary?"

I suppose I should have tumbled, but Laurel was saying, "Sometimes you make me want to strangle you," and I, remembering, said, "You darn near did, Laurel," and then the conversation went in other directions.

She stared at me, smiled slowly. "So I did. I had my chance, didn't I? You're impossible, Shell. Let's go get breakfast."

"No, thanks — and don't flip again. It's just that I never feel like breakfast till lunch. You go ahead. I want to make a call, anyway."

"At this hour?"

That was right. It was only about an hour after dawn. I wanted to phone Mrs. Redstone, but it could wait for a little while longer. I'd meant to phone her from here last night, and ask her if she knew anything about Poupelle's gambling, or had heard any mention of Castle Norman, and a few other things, but last night I had been sidetracked.

Laurel said, "You'd better eat something. You might have a big day ahead of you."

"I've got a big day behind me. But maybe you're right. I'll toy with a strip of bacon."

"Come on, I'll give you something that'll make you feel good."

"You already have. But I'm game. After this morning, I can stomach anything."

She said impishly, "Even me?"

In mock shock I said, "Laurel!" but she had turned to go.

I followed her to the right of the Council Building, past the pool, in which three women stood in four feet of water, appearing to hang there on marvelous water wings, and into the building, which turned out to be the dining room — cafeteria-style.

I looked at the line of people getting their trays filled with food, all of them with their backs to me, and I said, "Laurel, I'm not sure I can go through with this."

There were a number of square tables filling the room, and she led me to one, told me to sit down, and said, "I'll bring you some good nourishing food. You just wait there."

I waited. I had the urge to get up and go about my business, but what does a detective do on a case at this time of morning? Besides, I was still weak. There were a number of things I meant to do today, and several places I meant to go, and maybe Laurel had been right about my needing some nourishment. I was pretty hungry, at that; ravenous for me. Come to think of it, I hadn't eaten any dinner last night, and during the night I'd used up all the calories from lunch.

Laurel moved down the line, glancing over her shoulder at me every once in a while, and every time she did I was staring straight at her. In a group of fifty well-dressed people at a party, she would have stood out like a nudist; here, among nudists, there were not words to describe the sensation that was Laurel.

She came back to the table balancing two trays, unloaded them, and then sat down across from me. She slid a bowl of some cereal in front of me. I shrugged, picked up a spoon, and had at it — for one bite.

"What kind of slop is this?"

"That's wheat germ."

"Germs?"

"Wheat germ. The germ of wheat. It's what they take out of white bread so it won't spoil or keep you alive. Eat it. It's good for you."

"Haven't you got some white bread without germs? Or maybe some old typhoid bacillus?"

"One's about as bad as the other. Eat it. It's got the whole B complex in it."

"Baby, I've got enough complexes already. Especially in this madhouse. I'll soon start foaming — "

"I mean vitamins. Eat it."

She was stern. I looked at her, then grinned. "Yes, Mother." But I ate it. Thought a lot of that girl.

There was also a glass of milk at my plate, so I gulped half of it and roared. "What's that!"

"Milk."

"Yeah. From a dead cow. Tell me true, now. What was that?"

She giggled. "Milk. Oh, it's got a little brewer's yeast and lecithin and powdered skim milk and wheat germ in it, and — "

"You mean it's poisoned?"

"No, silly. Drink it." She laughed, then sat smiling at me for a moment, "Shell, don't you want to be as strong as the rest of us?"

I could feel my lip lifting. I sneered at her. And I downed that milk from a dead cow. It almost downed me. But I won and said proudly, "Look. I did it. I did it."

Well, there was more ugly stuff scattered around before me, but I was through. Laurel swept daintily through enough food to feed a regiment of Shell Scotts, then said, "Shall we go?"

We went. During what Laurel laughingly referred to as breakfast, she had told me that the Council wanted to talk to me some more about the convention — which, I recalled, was supposed to get under way tomorrow. I said I'd be gone most, if not all, of the day and for her to see if she couldn't convince the Council she could brief me herself. I felt rather peculiar about that convention and my supposed part in it, since I was quite sure I wouldn't be around. But there was always a chance that the wires I'd sent and the phone calls I'd made, plus the intensive work the Los Angeles police were putting in on the Yates homicide, would bear fruit. If so, my job for Mrs. Redstone could well be wound up today, in which case I'd be on my own time. And, anyway, I'd worry about tomorrow when it came.

There were no phones in the cabins, but Laurel reminded me of the phone in the Council Room. I told her I'd see her later and she gave me a resigned look, then went to her cabin. I found the phone in the empty Council Room, dialed Mrs. Redstone's number.

It rang for quite a while. I was thinking I should have called even later, since Mrs. Redstone was probably sound asleep. But she impressed me as a pretty fine party, who would pretend to be glad I'd awakened her even if she felt like yanking out the phone, so I let it go on ringing. That's exactly what it did; it went on ringing. Nobody answered.

That was funny, I thought. She'd hardly be out this early. Just in case I'd dialed the wrong number, I looked it up and carefully dialed it again, but there was still no answer. I hung up, then headed for my cabin. I knew there was probably no reason to hurry, but I ran anyway.

About half an hour later I arrived at the Redstone house, fully dressed up to the Colt Special under my coat. The curving white gravel drive was empty now, and I drove past the spot where I'd clobbered Garlic and parked before the cement steps. The front door was open. I rang several times, then went on inside.

I called a couple of times, but got no answer. I prowled around downstairs and then went up to the second floor.

I found her in a bedroom, wearing a quilted robe and seated in an overstuffed chair. I had been right back there at the camp: There'd been no need to hurry. Mrs. Redstone was sound asleep.

There was never a sounder sleep, never a more lasting or final sleep. She wouldn't wake up from this one. The vibrant, healthy, and in a way lovely Mrs. Redstone was dead, her skull quite shattered.

12

For a minute or so I just looked at her, feeling sicker and more sorry than I'd ever felt before in the presence of death, with very few exceptions. I hadn't been close to Mrs. Redstone, I had hardly known her, but she had been, I thought, a rare kind of woman. Strong, firm, pleasant. Intelligent and graceful. And, hell, I'd enjoyed her. I'd liked her. Not to mention the fact that she'd hired me to do a job for her. While I'd been jumping around at Fairview she must have been lying here dead.

Well, I'd finish the case for her, finish it for sure. And a hell of a lot of good that would do her now.

I went to her finally, touched her skin, looked at her dead eyes. *Rigor mortis* was just starting; it had affected the head and neck, but hadn't spread farther. She'd been dead for hours. On the floor at her feet, as if it might have fallen from her hand to her lap and then to the carpet, was a small, gleaming .32 Smith and Wesson revolver. Resting on a table to her left was a newspaper, still folded in the middle, the headlines spattered with brown stains and darker blobs.

The headlines were a surprise, and for a moment they didn't make much sense. Then they did. "Society Beauty Discovered in Nudist Camp." In smaller type at the head of a story covering the two right-hand columns was: "Daughter of Mrs. Ellen Redstone, Society Leader, Queen of Sunbathing Group."

I skimmed quickly through what I could see of the story without touching the paper, then spotted a phone, went to it, and dialed the complaint board at City Hall. I got put through to Samson in Homicide.

"Shell?" he said. "What's the idea of bothering a man who's just got to work?"

"Sam," I said, "remember Mrs. Redstone, gal who called you a couple of nights back?"

"Yeah. One you're working for, huh?"

"I was. She's dead, Sam. Murdered in her home. I'm at the place now."

He swore, asked me some questions, then said, "What makes you think she was killed?"

"A lot of things. It's set up to look like suicide, but it won't fit this one. Not for me it won't, anyway. It looks good, gun at her feet and all, but I can't buy it." I described the scene. He hadn't seen the *Clarion,* which had printed the story Mrs. Redstone had supposedly read, but I heard him yell to somebody to grab a copy and bring it up.

"Listen, Sam," I said. "There's a good chance this ties into the Yates homicide. And now might be the right time to ask the brand-new son-in-law, Andon Poupelle, where he was all night. I think the two daughters inherit fifteen-plus millions, and that leaves Poupelle in the middle of plenty of cash."

"Right, Shell. Thanks."

"Can you run down that *Clarion* story?"

"Yeah. Talk to Jim Hansen of the Wilshire Division when he gets out there. Call me back." He hung up.

I was careful where I put my feet as I walked back near Mrs. Redstone's body, bent over, and read the first part of the *Clarion's* article again. It was written in a flamboyant, lurid style that hinted at all sorts of dark and evil orgies. Sydney Laurel Redstone was named in the first line of the first paragraph, but I didn't see the name of the camp anywhere. I went downstairs and smoked a cigarette while I waited for the police cars and the dead wagon. I also thought quite a bit about Poupelle and Vera, Ed Norman and Paul Yates. And about Laurel, too.

A radio car was the first to arrive, with no siren. Right behind it came two Homicide detectives and Lieutenant James Hansen in a black Chrysler. I led them all upstairs, described everything I'd done since my arrival.

When the Homicide men and the crew from the crime lab got busy, Hansen took me out into the upstairs hall and said, "You were doing a job for her, Scott?"

"That's right." I gave him all I had that seemed important.

He frowned and said, "Her daughter's in a nudist camp?"

"Place called Fairview. Few miles out of town."

Hansen shrugged. "Looks to me like the old lady lamped that story and couldn't take it. She's big society stuff, you know. That kind of thing wouldn't ever die down. How come you don't see it that way, Scott?"

"I told you, Hansen, Mrs. Redstone knew her daughter was there. And she wasn't the type to go off her rocker over this thing, anyway."

He shrugged. Then he leered. "No kidding, Scott," he said. "This young daughter of hers is in a real nudist camp? Running around nekkid?"

"Yeah," I said. "No kidding."

I wasn't angry with him for getting a small kick out of the idea. I didn't know Hansen well, but I liked him. He was efficient, honest, worked fourteen hours a day most days, and he'd seen more dead men and women then I ever would. Once they were dead, they were just corpses, another job. But Hansen's reaction made me more aware of what other reactions would be.

He was a good cop, used to murders, and murders faked to look like suicide. And he didn't think this one had been phonied. He was mildly worried because it was such a big one, and mildly amused at the circumstances surrounding it. I remembered what I'd thought yesterday after that shot at me out at Fairview: that if I *had* been knocked off, the emphasis wouldn't have been on "murder," but on "nudist camp." For the first time I began to consider the possibility that I might even wind up alone in thinking Mrs. Redstone had been murdered.

I said, "Give her a paraffin test, anyway."

"Sure," he said. "We'll cover it six ways from the middle. You're really bugs on the idea she didn't do it, aren't you?" He paused. "That's right, you were working for the gal. What's the matter? Now she's dead, you feel — "

"I don't feel anything. Just slip that paraffin glove on her and find out if she fired a gun."

He nodded. "Well, I guess we better talk to the daughter."

That was right, Laurel couldn't know about this yet. Nor, for that matter, would Vera. Except for me and the police, probably only the killer knew. I said, "Hansen, let me tell her."

He frowned and was silent for a while. Then he said, "Can't hurt. All right."

"OK if I phone her from here?"

"Go ahead. Don't tell her what it's about."

"I'll just tell her I've got some bad news."

Mrs. Redstone's body was being carried downstairs to the dead wagon as we went back into the bedroom. Lieutenant Hansen said to the tall, gray-haired coroner's deputy, "When'd it happen?"

The man stopped. "Around midnight, I'd say. Roughly — very roughly. Let you know more later, Jim." He went out.

Hansen stood near me as I dialed the number of the phone in Fairview's Council Room. A man answered.

"Who's this?" I asked him.

"Bob Brown. Who's calling?"

"Scott. Don Scott."

"Ah, the energetic health director. What can I do for you?"

"Put Laurel Redstone on the line, will you?"

There was silence for a few minutes, then Laurel's soft voice said, "Mr. Scott?"

"Yeah. Laurel, uh, anything new happen?"

"No. You sound strange."

"Get into a . . . different outfit, and meet me at the gate in about twenty minutes." Hansen chuckled softly when I said "different outfit."

Laurel said slowly, "All right. What's the matter?"

"I've got some bad news for you. Lousy news."

"What is it?"

"I'll tell you when I see you. I'm coming out with some police officers. They'll probably want to talk to you too."

"Police? What is it? What *is* it?"

"Can't tell you right now, Laurel. See you in a little while."

She said all right and we hung up.

Hansen said, "Let's go."

Laurel was waiting outside the gate when Hansen, a detective sergeant, and I drove up in an official car. She looked fresh and young as a spring morning in a simple white dress, unadorned except for a brown belt. She was carrying a brown bag and wearing low-heeled shoes, and a worried expression was on her face. When the car stopped I got out and went over to her, Hansen following close behind me.

She put her hand on my arm, looked beyond me to Hansen. "Shell, what's the matter? You sounded so — so grim on the phone."

I knew she'd had all the time since I'd phoned to get ready for what I was going to say, but I still couldn't come right out with it. I said, "Laurel, this gentleman is Detective Lieutenant Hansen, of Homicide."

"Homicide?" she said. "Why is he — "

I swallowed. "Laurel, your mother is dead."

She looked blankly at me, then smiled slowly. "Stop it, Shell. This isn't a very good joke."

"It isn't a joke. It looked like suicide, but — anyway, she was shot. She's dead, Laurel. I found her body."

Her expression was still blank. "I don't believe it," she said. "I won't believe it until . . . I see her."

Hansen stepped forward then and began to talk to Laurel. He told her it was just routine, and asked her if she'd been in camp all night. She said she had been and, yes, she could prove it. For most of the night, anyway. She looked at me then. She corroborated the fact that she and her sister, Vera, would inherit her mother's estate. But she still wasn't believing us when she got into the police car and we drove away.

On the way into town I showed Laurel a copy of the *Clarion*, which Hansen had picked up, but it just bounced off her. I'd finished reading the story on the way to Fairview. We drove in silence.

The L.A. county morgue is downstairs in the Hall of Justice. We parked in the Spring Street lot and Laurel, Hansen, and I went inside, leaving the sergeant at the wheel of the car. Inside the Hall of Justice we turned left, went past the door marked "Coroner," and on down to the end of the hall. At our left was Room 106, our first stop, but before we went in I glanced to the right, down another short hall to the door marked "Viewing Room." Mrs. Redstone's body would be in there now, beyond that door.

In a minute or two Laurel had identified herself and we all walked toward the Viewing Room, one of the men from the Coroner's Office with us. It was quiet and I held Laurel's arm as we walked. Her muscles were stiff under my fingers and her face had a frozen, almost deathlike look.

It was over in a few seconds, but it seemed like a year to me. It must have seemed longer to Laurel. We stepped into the small room and I turned Laurel gently to her left. Just behind the thick plate-glass window, resting on its four-wheeled table and covered with a chenille bedspread, was Mrs. Redstone's body.

The spread hid the table, covered everything except the profile of that dead face. Hansen said in a quiet voice, "This is your mother, isn't it, Miss Redstone?"

His voice was soft and gentle, but here in the small room and with that lifeless body only a yard from us, the words sounded hollow, and as brutal as a hammer against a coffin.

"Why, yes," Laurel said. "Yes."

She looked at me, face blank, eyes dull. "It is Mother, Shell." No outcry, no tears. She turned and went out the door, started back down the hall. She walked slowly and stiffly, putting one foot before the other with exaggerated care, like a woman walking after weeks in bed. I stayed alongside her, my hand on her arm.

Hansen looked at his watch as we reached the car. I said, "You don't need either of us now, do you?"

"Not now. Later I'll want to see both of you."
"Sure. I'll be in touch. We'll grab a cab if it's all right with you."
He glanced at Laurel, chewed on his lip, and nodded. "The girl — she'll be OK, won't she?"
"I'll stick with her as long as she wants me to."
He nodded and left. We walked to the corner and caught a cab. Inside, I said, "Where do you want to go, Laurel?"
She looked at me. "Home, I guess." I tried to talk her out of going there, but she was insistent. I leaned forward and gave the driver the address of the Redstone house, then sat back. Laurel kept looking at me. She said, "I just want to go home. But there isn't anybody there now, is there? Nobody there."
The frozen look melted. She said in a hardly audible whisper, "Oh-h . . . oh, my God!" And then the tears came. She threw herself forward against my chest, head burrowing hard against me, her hands balled into small fists pressed on each side of her face, and great shaking sobs racked her body. I put my arms around her and held her, but I couldn't think of anything to say that would make it easier for her. There wasn't anything to say.
She stayed like that for the rest of the ride, but slowly the sobs subsided. When the cab stopped in the graveled drive she pushed herself away from me, fumbled in her bag for a handkerchief, and wiped some of the tears and mascara streaks from her face. I paid the driver and we went inside the house.
I guess I spent about half an hour with Laurel. She asked me to tell her the whole thing again. I'd learned that the .32 Smith and Wesson had been Mrs. Redstone's own gun, and finally I said, "Honey, do you think she could have . . . "
Laurel was under control now, dry-eyed and sober. "Killed herself?" she said. "That's idiotic. She was murdered. She wouldn't have, couldn't have killed herself. My God, Shell, who would do a thing like that? And why? Why?"
She didn't expect an answer, and I didn't have any to give her. I did try to convince her again that she should stay somewhere else, even mentioned that my apartment might be safer, but she said she wanted to be alone here for a while. In a few minutes she asked me to go.
I hesitated and Laurel said, "Go ahead, Shell. Thanks, but I'll be all right. I just don't want to talk, or see anyone, or anything."
I got up to leave and she came over to me.
"Put your arms around me, Shell. Don't kiss me, just hold me a minute. Just hold me."

She pressed close against me, then turned and walked away. I went out. My Cad was still in the drive. I'd left it here when I'd gone with Hansen to Fairview. I started it and headed for downtown Los Angeles. There was a man I meant to find. A murderer; maybe a guy after a lot of money. Maybe even a woman. But I had to learn quite a bit more today, had to be sure I got my hands on the right guy. Because when I found him, I might kill him.

13

Samson had his cigar going when I walked into Homicide in City Hall, but I made no cracks about his weeds today.

He looked up and saw me, then growled around his cigar, "Shell, glad you came down. We got something you're interested in. Some dope on Poupelle just came in from Washington." He reached for some papers on his desk, saying. "What's with the Redstone woman? You saw Hansen, didn't you?"

"Yeah. Just left him a while back." I briefed him on the high points of what had happened, then looked over the papers he'd given me. While I glanced at them he covered the salient points, punctuating his words with streams of foul cigar smoke.

"This Poupelle's a grade-A louse. Mixed up in a kind of badger game in Cincinnati, also Philadelphia. Only instead of a shapely babe and a furious husband, Poupelle played the babe's part and arranged for a house dick to catch him with the gals. The women paid off the detective, who split with Poupelle."

"He did time?"

"No, that's the sweet angle of his racket. He picked his female patsies from the real upper crust, gals from the local high society. Babes afraid their society laying would hurt their society standing, and wouldn't finger the bastard. Charges brought once in Cincy, once in Philly — and both times the complaining witnesses blew cold, dropped the complaints. So, as far as we can tell, he wasn't ever convicted of a crime."

I grinned at Sam. "Maybe I'll convict the bum, when I get my hands on him. You talk to him yet?"

He nodded. "Yeah, we brought in him and the wife, Vera. In case you were wondering, they've got airtight alibis. They were with this Ed Norman you mentioned last night, and half a dozen other people. Out at that castle. Until a couple of hours after the place closed, by the way."

"So that means all three of them, plus half a dozen other people, have alibis. But, Sam, a guy could leave the castle, knock somebody off, then come back in. Probably with nobody the wiser. You know, everybody drinking, wandering around. Wouldn't have to be gone over an hour. Probably a lot less."

"Well, the story hangs together. Besides, all we could do was question them, easy like. There's no complaint or anything against them."

"How'd Vera take it?"

"Went all to pieces. We let her lie down here a while before they left."

I ran through the rest of the report, most of which Samson had given me verbally. "This dope fits Poupelle like a boy's BVDs, Sam. Wherever there's big money and women starting downhill, you find slobs like Poupelle hanging around giving them a push. Always a friend of a friend, guys with maybe one or two talents, neither of which is polo, but they make a good living. I kind of had a hunch about Andon. I've got some more hunches about him, too. Something about those alibis smells."

"Sure. Could be they're all lying. Or just some of them are lying. We can't put thumbscrews on them. Anything else bring you down?"

I reached into my pocket. On the way here I'd stopped by my apartment, changed clothes, and got the original report that Paul Yates had given Mrs. Redstone. A couple of telegrams had also arrived for me and I'd picked those up just before coming to City Hall. "You've answered some of it already, Sam. But chew on this."

I gave him the typed report and the two wires. "Vera told me Poupelle was some kind of broker in New York, but nobody there ever heard of him, witness wire one. The other wire's from the Kellogg agency in New York. They're doing some checking for me and, so far, got a line on Poupelle's Cincinnati activities. That was enough to bring me here — but you're way ahead of me."

"Naturally."

"Anyway, it seems Vera doesn't know her hubby's background very well. I don't say she doesn't; I say she says she doesn't. And look over the result of

Yates's investigation of Poupelle. You and I both got a little on him in practically no time; but not Yates. Not a word in his report about Andon's being a loverboy, nothing damaging or derogatory. It's all phony — and it all smells worse than your cigars."

"These are good cigars. The stuff we got just came in, so we weren't able to ask Poupelle about all this. We will — and he can be amazed. You can't ask Yates."

"True. Something else I wanted to talk to you about. I imagine you've gone over Yates's stuff pretty closely. Home, office, so on."

"Right. Didn't tell us anything. Might look a little different now."

"That's what I mean. I'd like to go over his files this afternoon. And I want to check Poupelle's bank account. Can you fix it for me?"

Sam nodded and rolled gray ash off his cigar "Stuff's still in Yates's office. We went through it there. Eighth and Hill. I've got a man there, Sergeant Billings, just to keep an eye open, but I'll tell him you're coming down. And I can get you into his bank, probably. California on Spring Street. What do you expect to find?"

"I dunno, Sam. On the bank angle, I learned Poupelle dropped a big wad at Castle Norman, passed a bum check for it. Might find a record of it. Might not. And there's a screwy Norman-Poupelle relationship in this thing." I paused a moment, then went on. "There's another idea floating around in my head. Suppose Poupelle knocked off somebody and Norman found out about it and started bleeding Poupelle. I mean, quite a while back. Might explain a couple of things."

"It might. Might not. Why would Norman blackmail Poupelle? I imagine Norman's got plenty of cash; Poupelle's not loaded."

"Not then he wouldn't have been, maybe. He sure is now."

Sam took the cigar from his wide mouth, deliberately ground it out. "Yeah. This'll kill you. Those hard boys that jumped you yesterday at that night club — all four of them work for Ed Norman."

I didn't say anything for quite a while. Then I got up and walked to the wall of his cramped office, leaned against it. "Sam, here's a short paragraph. See how it reads. Poupelle comes out to the Coast, and his character doesn't improve like the weather, he stays a bastard. He drops a wad at Castle Norman, gives Norman a rubber check. Around the same period he wiggles up to the Redstone clan. Mrs. Redstone adds him up and gets the correct answer: Zero. Puts an investigator — Yates — on his educated tail. Yates fakes a report for Mrs. Redstone, but Yates isn't so thick he doesn't know quite a bit about Poupelle's background, just as we do. Say Poupelle is working his racket, or even wants to marry into a pile of bucks. If Yates spills the real beans to Mrs. Redstone, Poupelle's party is a bust." I stopped.

Sam scowled. "So?"

"Yates is dead, isn't he?"

"That he is. Fits all right, Shell. Could be." He scowled some more. "So is Mrs. Redstone dead. But she maybe blew her think pot herself."

"Maybe good little girls go to heaven. Come off it, Sam. You don't think she did it."

"I don't know what I think, Shell. I'm not a private dick that guesses right all the time and prowls around nudist parks. I'm a cop, and I got to have more than guesses."

"Nudist! Why, that fiend Hansen! He tell you that, Sam?"

"He did." Sam chuckled and stuck a new cigar in his chops. It occurred to me that if Sam knew the whole story about me and that nudist park, he might swallow his cigar and strangle on it.

"So I'm uninhibited," I said, and changed the subject. "It seems peculiar that Ed Norman's name crops up so often. He's the boy who was chinning with Garlic night before last." I told Sam about my conversation with Norman at the castle. "As for Poupelle, maybe he needed money bad. You don't welsh on guys like Norman, much less slap them with rubber paper."

Sam said, "On that forty-five of Garlic's. We ran it through SID, got nothing. New gun."

"Makes sense. He probably throws the old guns away whenever he kills somebody." I lit a cigarette and said casually, "A guy took a shot at me yesterday, and I think there's a fifty-fifty chance the slug was from a gun that wasn't thrown away, from the rifle that kissed Yates off."

Sam was doodling on his pad, but he dropped the pencil and jerked his head up. "What? This is a *fine* time to be telling me. For Christ's sake, Shell, you gonna keep it a secret till they tie a tag on your toe in the morgue?"

"He missed me."

"Where was this? How about that bullet?"

I was damned if I'd tell him where it was; not just yet, anyway. As long as that tag stayed off my toe, I figured to be working closely and congenially with Sam and the rest of the guys at headquarters. I had seen the gleam in Hansen's eye, read the *Clarion*'s sly insinuations and not-so-subtle innuendoes about "sunbathers" and "naturists," and I had sensed Sam inner glee at the thought of my merely being *near* a nudist camp. If the truth were ever known, Sam would ride me practically into the morgue all by himself. And I quailed at the thought of what the rest of my pals scattered over all twenty-eight stories of City Hall would do with so juicy an item.

I said to Samson, "It was out of town. The slug's in an absolutely impossible place, up high on the side of a scooped-out cliff. Take my word for it."

"Why not have the boys take a look at it? If there's any chance it is from the Yates gun — which we haven't any trace of — that bullet might be damned important."

"Sam, it's inaccessible. I know how important it might be. But you can't get at it with a ladder or even fire-department paraphernalia. You'd have to overcome the forces of gravity to get it, and I'm not that clever. Besides, it might not even have been a thirty-thirty."

A crazy idea skittered in my brain. I remembered telling Laurel that the only way to get up that outward slanting cliff would be to float up. It was still a goofy idea, but I let it bubble in my head while I kept talking to Sam. "How about Bender, the con boy I mentioned yesterday."

"Got a little, not much. He's part of the bunch that hangs out at the club, that Afrodite. But he hasn't been seen around there lately."

"Since when?"

"Since a month ago. Last time we've placed him there was on June first. Then he disappeared. And there's no connection at all with Poupelle."

"How about with Norman? He wasn't one of Norman's boys like Foo and Strikes and the rest, was he?"

"No sign of it. Free-lance. Self-employed except when he tied up with another con and they both took a mark for his roll."

"How'd he work? Anything there?"

"Yeah, he's got a record here and over half the country." Sam dug into his desk, found a sheet of paper. "Last couple, three years, he's been working the wire mostly. He's a cackle-bladder expert, too. During the last Santa Anita season he was in with Good Time Wilson, had a store out on Eighty-ninth Street; they took Fowler, of Fowler, Brandt, and Parker, right there in the store, for eighty-five thousand on some rigged race horses. You'd think a lawyer would know better."

"Not if he got the itch, and a good con boy can give angels the itch. The marks see those thousand-dollar bills."

Sam's men had checked on the *Clarion* article, talked to the reporter who'd written it. The reporter's story was that he'd received an anonymous phone call yesterday, giving details about Laurel Redstone's nudism kick, plus a suggestion that he look in his mailbox, which he did. There he'd found an envelope containing information that satisfied him, plus a couple of pictures, probably taken with a telephoto lens, of Laurel and others in the camp. He'd got his story written barely in time to make the late edition. He wouldn't say what the other information was, pointing out that the important fact was that his article was true, and insisted the phone call had been anonymous. I didn't believe it, of course, but Sam's men had to be content with that much.

That was about all Samson could tell me. He made phone calls to Yates's office and the California Bank, hung up, and told me it was all set. "Ed Norman has an account there, too, if that does you any good."

"It might." I went to the door. "Thanks, Sam. When you get Poupelle again, I'd like to talk with him."

"Sure. Don't get killed."

"Not a chance. I'll call you before you knock off."

I phoned him sooner than I'd expected to, though. And I almost got that tag on my toe.

14

When I left City Hall, I climbed into the convertible and drove to a gas station, where I used the pay phone to call a friend of mine named Jay Carter, a dealer in government surplus from whom I'd bought a couple of thousand dollars' worth of equipment in the past.

I recognized his secretary's slightly nasal voice when she answered, "Carter's Surplus, anything for a price."

"What can I get for a martini?"

"Shell! Where've you been? You horrid thing." Maybe her voice was a little nasal, but the rest of her was virtually without flaw.

"Hi, Sally. Can you put Carter on for me? I'm in a hurry this afternoon."

"Instead of putting Carter on, wouldn't you rather — "

"Sally, I said I was in a hurry."

"Well, nuts to you."

The phone went onto a desktop with a clatter. In a moment Carter bawled into it. We yakked a minute, then I told him what I wanted.

"What in Christ's name are you up to now?" he asked me.

"Never mind. Just get it and don't boost the price more than a thousand percent."

"You know me. I can get it — and cheap — especially for you, my fran', but what in Christ's — "

"You wouldn't believe me. How soon?"

"Couple days OK?"

"No. I want the stuff this afternoon."

"Impossible."

"I hear the price going up. OK, Jay, just get it."

"Well . . . " He was quiet for a minute. "Most of it I got. Give me eight hours. That's the best, Shell."

It was eleven A.M. now. "All right, Jay," I said "Do the best you can, and throw in a Coleman lantern."

"Will do. But what in Christ's name are you — "

I hung up on him and headed for the California Bank. The manager wasn't delighted at the prospect of letting me peek at his books and microfilms. They never are. But Sam had talked to him, and in a few minutes I was seated at the viewer of a big Recordak, looking at the projected images of Andon Poupelle's checks. A male clerk, who would help me with other records of deposits and withdrawals, operated the Recordak, flashing the enlarged images of check after check on the white screen. While I was at it I gave Ed Norman's account a going-over, too. When I got through I wasn't sure I'd learned anything new — but I had found the microfilm of a check dated May 28 of this year, signed Andon Poupelle and made out to Edward Norman. It was in the amount of $56,000 and had been sent back to the endorser, Norman, with a notation that it was being returned because of insufficient funds in Poupelle's account.

Norman hadn't been too helpful last night, but at least Three Eyes had given me the straight dope on that item; and he was the man who'd also told me there was a rumble that Poupelle had pushed one Bender. Bender, who hadn't been seen around for a month.

Ed Norman's account showed several deposits of about five or ten thousand dollars, and similar withdrawals every few days. On the fifteenth of each month a check in the amount of $100,000 had been made out by Edward Norman to something called General Enterprises, Inc.

Norman seemed to be skating pretty close to the edge of his account. The latest $100,000 check had been made out when his balance was $33,000, but two days later, on June 17, he'd deposited $150,000 in cash. He had a savings account, too, but there was little in it.

The last thing I did was check bank balances. Ed Norman's totaled $64,000; Poupelle's — which until just recently had never been higher than

$4,200 — had jumped to a current $12,000, which wasn't tremendously interesting information. And I know it was sneaky of me, but I learned that Vera Poupelle had her account here, and I peeked at it, then wished I hadn't. It was probably just her mad money, but it totaled $468,533 and some pennies. That finished me. I left.

I started back over the same route I'd taken yesterday, the bars and the back rooms, lower Hill, Main Street. I talked to an usher in the Follies Theatre, and wasted a whole minute admiring the life-sized photos of Merry Cherry Blame, the Madwoman of Burlesque. I talked to a couple of barbers, some winos, several hoodlums, a bookie. I got nothing but sore feet and a burning curiosity about Merry Cherry Blaine.

I did pick up one interesting little item, though. I learned that a few months back Ed Norman hired a press agent to boom Castle Norman, so I looked the guy up and talked to him for ten minutes. It seemed that the castle had been pretty much of a bust and was losing money until the "publicity consultant," as he called himself, took over and made a few changes. He'd had Norman put the wall around the castle, add the fake moat and the drawbridge and dress the help in twentieth-century armor, and so on.

The upshot was that business had picked up. The press agent's final advice to Norman had been that he double the prices of everything so the customers would feel they were getting something good. Maybe a moral was in there somewhere.

At two in the afternoon I was in my office. The guppies were fed, I'd made eleven phone calls, and I was staring at the phone when it came to life and rang. I grabbed it and a wheezy voice said, "Scott?"

"Yeah. Who's this?"

"Papa. You talked to me yesterday at Coco's. I picked up something there last night. Been tryin' to catch you."

Coco's was a fairly pleasant bar down Broadway, where a lot of hoods drank when they had a few bucks; when the bucks melted, they slipped down to beer and port at one of the joints like Jerry's, where I'd talked to Iggy the Wig yesterday. The wheezy-voiced guy on the phone now would be a rummy named Papa Garden; I'd offered him a little cash for any help he could throw my way. We'd traded money for information before. Some of it had been good.

"What's up?"

"About Poupelle. You stirred up a lot of the boys yesterday and today, didn't you? There's a lot of talk, but nobody's saying anything. Except this noise I heard. It don't sound like much, but the word was Poupelle got a loan. From Offie."

I whistled. This Offie was an old man named Offenbach, or Offenheimer or something like that. Guesses about what he was worth started at twenty or thirty million and went up astronomically. He was older than the Grand Canyon, according to what I'd heard, and his one interest was making money to pile on top of his money.

Offie was so rich that his purpose in making more dough wasn't merely the idea of getting richer, but the kick he got from the deals themselves. Offie didn't care whether the deal was legal or illegal, just so it was possible and there'd be a fat profit in it for Offie. Adding another million now and then was just sort of a pleasant hobby with him.

I said, "A loan, huh? Then it would have been big."

"With Offie it wouldn't of been nickels."

"When did it happen?"

"Dunno. Like I said, it's nothin', Scott. But I thought maybe. Well, you know. I thought maybe . . . "

"Don't burst into tears. You didn't make this up, did you?"

"Christ, no. I swear it. I heard it."

"Where? And when?"

"I don't remember so good. I'd had . . . a glass of beer. Two beers, in fact." He paused. "Is it good for a fin?"

His voice was anxious. I figured he was broke and had a hangover, a horrible combination. "It's worth that," I said. "Twice that if you remember where and when and who. I need that info."

"Well, it was in Coco's last night. Sometime. I think it was Three Eyes sounding off. He wasn't talking to me, but I was at the bar near him. I ain't sure, Scott."

"Three Eyes? I thought he blew town."

"Nah. He was around last night anyways."

"I'll have to chat again with the guy. Who else was there?"

"I dunno. I told you I had a beer. Two beers."

"You get the ten. Where are you?"

"Jerry's."

"See you there in about five minutes." I hung up. It was almost five minutes, though, before I left the office, because I sat at my desk thinking about what Papa had said for nearly that long. And a couple of items melted together in my mind. June 17 was one of the dates I'd noted in the California Bank's records. This was July 2. I counted back two days, to the time I'd been hired, then back another two weeks, which brought me to June 16. That was one day off, and just right, I thought. The date had seemed a little familiar. I picked up the phone again and dialed the number of the Redstone house. In a minute Laurel answered. "This is Shell," I said. "Everything all right, honey?"

"Hello, Shell. I'm glad you called. Everything's all right. Anyway, it's the same."

"How do you feel?"

"Well enough. I'm over the bad part. Now that I believe it happened." She was quiet for a moment. "Mother and I hadn't been really close for years. But . . . I guess we were closer than I thought. Funny, isn't it? I think I'll go back to Fairview, Shell. I can't stand it here at the house now alone."

"Don't go back to Fairview unless I'm with you, Laurel. OK?"

"I guess. Why, Shell?"

"Might be safer. Look, honey, I want to ask you something. When were Vera and Andon married?"

"June 16."

"Morning or afternoon?"

"Afternoon, four o'clock."

She said something else, but I wasn't listening. I'd thought they'd been hitched on the sixteenth. It was just right; the banks would have been closed at four P.M. Laurel went on, "If you don't want me to go back to Fairview, let me join you, be with you."

"I'd enjoy that, but I'll be busy for a while."

"What are you doing?"

"I've got to talk with a guy that gave me some info. Then I'm going to rummage around a detective's office."

"What detective's office?"

"Yates, Paul Yates. I asked you about him a time or two."

"I'd like to be with you, Shell. Can't I — "

"You wouldn't enjoy it. I'll be busy. I'll pick you up later this afternoon."

"But I can't stay here. It's depressing. I could meet — "

"Look, I'm not sure what I'll run into. Just as soon as I can, I'll drive out. And don't go back to Fairview."

I told her good-bye and hung up, then drove to Jerry's. Papa grabbed my ten-dollar bill as if it were already twenty shots of bourbon, but he couldn't add anything to what he'd told me on the phone, except the address of the place where Three Eyes was staying. I left him and headed for Three Eyes' room in the Manor Hotel, which sounded like a grand place to live, at a dollar a day, with bath down the hall.

I parked around the corner and walked in, past an aged bewhiskered desk clerk, and up rickety wooden stairs, wondering if Three Eyes had purposely left the item about Poupelle's fat loan out of the info he'd given me, or if he'd just forgotten it. Maybe he'd picked it up after I'd given him that hundred, which he'd immediately started spending in Coco's. Spending for tongue-loosening liquor. I hoped he was home, and I hoped he was sober.

Three Eyes shacked in Room 27, up one flight and halfway down a dark, gloomy hall that smelled of mildew and worse. I knocked a couple of times but there wasn't any answer. After the sound of my knuckles on the wooden door, the silence seemed to increase. The entire hotel was quiet, only noise from the streets outside filtering in here.

I started to go back down to the desk, then tried the door. The knob turned and the door opened. Apparently Three Eyes hadn't even locked himself in. Maybe he hadn't been as nervous and jumpy as he'd pretended. I started to push the door wider, and it hit something with a light click. After that click there was another odd sound I couldn't place at first.

It was like something rolling, like a marble rolling over the uncarpeted floor. Then the hair moved on the back of my neck. Coldness shivered along my spine. The thing inside hit something, a table or a chair leg or the wall, then rolled a little farther and stopped. Even before I went inside I knew what it was.

It was an eye.

15

I swung the door open and stepped inside, shutting it behind me. I saw the glass eye immediately, across the room from me. Its whiteness stood out even in the gloom, the artificial iris nearly hidden against the floor.

Three Eyes was crumpled against the left wall, in the corner of the room. He lay on his back, twisted, his face battered, the empty socket like the hole in a skull. His face was bloody — and cold. He had been dead for quite a while.

Three Eyes had been a small man, but he had fought for his life. The room was a shambles. His clothing was torn and the fingertips of his left hand were stained with somebody's blood. I turned away. There are few sights uglier than the face of a man who has been choked to death.

The bed was mussed and torn. It looked as if Three Eyes had been in bed when it happened, when it had started to happen. I thought of him lying there in darkness as the door opened and somebody came in, walked toward him, and I shivered slightly. I glanced around at the room once more, then went downstairs to the desk.

The old clerk looked at me with empty eyes.

I said, "Three Eyes in?"

He scratched the gray stubble on his cheek and shrugged.

"You know who I'm talking about, don't you? Room Twenty-seven."

"Yep. Dunno if'n he's in or not" Slowly he craned his head around and looked at the slots where the keys were kept. His eyes fell on the slot for Room 27 and he turned back to me. It seemed to take forever.

"Yep. He's in."

"He have any visitors last night or this morning?"

"Dunno."

"Anybody else at the desk last night besides you?"

"Nope. Just me. Sometimes I sleep and you got to ring the bell." He started to point at the bell, but long before his quivering finger completed the journey I gave up on him.

"Can I use your phone?" I said.

"Yep." His finger started waggling toward the phone, but I beat him again and put in a call to Samson.

I gave him the picture. "That's it. Soon as your boys get here and look the place over, I'm taking off, unless they need me. I only found the guy. And I've got plenty of things to do."

"Go ahead, Shell. You think it ties in?"

"Yeah. Looks like somebody's getting scared."

"Watch that big toe of yours."

"Sure. See you." I hung up and got outside as a gray Ford coupé with a banged-up front fender started to pull in to the curb; it pulled out again as the police buggy stopped. After ten minutes I was through with the police and ready to leave again.

Before leaving the hotel I used a phone book to look up General Enterprises, Incorporated. It wasn't listed, which seemed odd to me.

It didn't take long to find out where Offie did business when he was available. He had a suite of offices on Sunset Boulevard near Van Ness, in a modern, pink-stucco building set back behind green lawn bisected by a white sidewalk. I went up to the door and into expensively refrigerated air. Nothing but the best for Offie — and that included a peach of a receptionist

She was wearing a dark skirt, above which was a pink sweater she might have knitted herself, getting halfway through with the job before saying the hell with it. Offie was so old I figured she was on display for the customers. I got younger every minute. She was strategically seated, so that she smacked you in the eyes when you entered, and she was strategically built so that she smacked you in *both* eyes. Hell, she smacked you all over.

She smiled at me, and I looked around the reception room, figuring I'd better look at it now if I was ever going to. Closed doors, with plain frosted-glass windows, studded the left and right walls. That told me nothing, so I looked back at the gal and walked up to her desk.

She wasn't a little girl, she wasn't little anywhere, and she wore grown-up clothes, but they hadn't grown up quite as much as she had. She looked like one of Cole's sensual women in *Playboy* magazine — blonde, with big brown eyes and those other big things you hear about but don't often see. At least don't often see so well. Not often enough, anyway.

"Good afternoo-oon," she crooned. "What can I do-oo for you?"

I came within half an inch of giving it to her straight. But I said, resolutely, "I'd like a few minutes with Offie."

She kept smiling. "Oh, you're a friend of Mr. Offenbrand's?"

"No, but I'm sure — "

"Your name?"

"Shell Scott."

She blinked. "Oh, *you're* Shell Scott. I've heard about you. But of course you're Shell Scott. Who else would you be?"

"You've got me there," I said brilliantly. "Who else, indeed?"

No telling to what conversational heights we might have risen, but then she said, "You don't have an appointment."

"No. It's all right, though. I'm sure he'll see me."

"I'm sure he won't. He never sees anybody without an appointment."

"I'll bet he sees you."

She rolled her big brown eyes around like Ferris wheels and giggled. "I'll bet. He's eighty-six, though." She giggled again, as if she knew something I didn't know. Undoubtedly she knew plenty I didn't know.

I said, "Well, then, honey, you just slide into his office and tell him *you're* out here and would like to see him. How's that?"

Her face got blank. "I don't believe I understand where you're driving at."

"Do this for me, will you, honey? Tell Offie that Shell Scott is here to see him. Tell him, further, it's about a man named Andon Poupelle. That might just do it."

She considered it, then stood up and pulled down the base of her pink sweater, the base being about all there was to pull on, and walked out from behind the desk. "All rightie," she said, and swayed toward the closed door on my right.

I had half a cigarette smoked by the time she came out again, fifteen seconds later. She sat down behind her desk, looked at me soberly, and said, "You were wrong. He won't, either, see you."

"We'll try one more time," I said. "Tell him that what I really want to see him about is General Enterprises, Incorporated. And about a bum check. Be sure to mention that the check is for one hundred thousand dollars."

She went into her act again, swaying gently to and fro as if she were listening to music that I couldn't hear. It must have been a slow rumba combined with a fast waltz. This time when she came out she stood by the open door and said, "You may come in, Mr. Scott."

That told me almost everything I'd wanted to know; but I went in anyway. Offenbrand was seated behind a coal-black desk about twelve feet wide. He was a small man, but somehow the desk didn't dwarf him, and if he was eighty-six he sure as hell didn't look it. Maybe that blonde wasn't for the customers, after all.

He stood up behind the desk, to about five feet, five or six inches, a dark-skinned guy with a full head of wavy white hair. "Mr. Scott," he said in a firm voice, and shook my hand with a grip just as firm. "Explain."

His eyes were black, fixed directly on mine, and they looked colder than frozen meatballs.

"How do you do, Mr. Offenbrand," I said. "I'll explain. That's why I came here." I looked around, found a leather chair, and sat down in it.

He got behind his desk again and looked at me, waiting. I said, "In return for my explanation, I'll expect a couple of answers myself. About Andon Poupelle, for one thing."

"Perhaps."

"OK. To start with, who operates General Enterprises?"

He didn't say anything.

I went on, "A man named Ed Norman pays General Enterprises a hundred grand a month. I don't know why for sure — maybe you can tell me — but I imagine it's principal and interest on a big loan. Say a million or so. The last check Norman made out to General Enterprises was written when he had thirty-three thousand in his checking account, four thousand in his savings account. Two days later, on June 17, he deposited a hundred and fifty thousand dollars. So the check didn't bounce. But for two days it was rubber. Interesting?"

"Extremely. If true, Mr. Scott."

"It's true. You head General Enterprises," I said. "I'm a detective, as I suppose you're aware. And part of the little I know about you is that you'd be damned disturbed if anybody played you for a sucker. In any way at all. And it begins to look, doesn't it, as if somebody played you for a sucker?"

He didn't say anything. His face just looked a little harder.

I said, "You'll make just as much — more this way, as a matter of fact — but it's still a sucker play. To you, I assume, the rub would be the way it was handled. Right? And maybe the next hundred thousand bounces. Am I making sense?"

He was quiet for another minute or so, then he nodded briskly as if he'd made up his mind about something. "Yes. Is that all?"

"That's all I've got. And you must realize I'm guessing at a lot of it, but it fits. All I want from you is to know if I've guessed right. I know Ed Norman pays General Enterprises a hundred grand a month. I've assumed that you control the company."

"I don't control it; I *am* General Enterprises. Mr. Norman needed money quickly for that club of his. He was then in the process of building it. I advanced him a million, two hundred."

"How about Andon Poupelle?"

"He wanted money, of course, half a million, but I never give a man all he wants. We settled the transaction so that he pays me two-fifty within a year. I make a hundred in that period, which is a fair profit."

When Offie said "a hundred," he meant a hundred thousand dollars; he talked about thousands like I do about quarters. Any way you looked at it, though, he meant he'd given Poupelle a hundred and fifty thousand clams.

I said, "It wouldn't have been a check, I don't suppose."

For a moment I thought he was going to smile. His lip twitched, then he said, "It was in cash. One of my men delivered it personally."

"Just one other thing, Mr. Offenbrand. What security did Mr. Poupelle have to offer?" I grinned at him. "Naturally I examined his bank account, too."

"Security enough. He told me he was marrying more than fifteen million dollars. He didn't receive any money from me until after the actual ceremony."

"And that was June 16."

"I believe so." I knew that was a date he'd be interested in too, now, so it didn't surprise me when he pressed a button on a squawk box near the corner of his desk and said, "Daphne. Poupelle. The date." In a moment her voice said from the box, "June 16."

"Just a thought," I said. "What if a man couldn't pay you back?"

The thought amused him. "Oh, they all pay, Mr. Scott. One way or another."

I got up. "Thanks, Mr. Offenbrand." I headed for the door.

Before I reached it he said, "Mr. Scott. Thank *you*. Your information was interesting. And it will also be interesting to see how this works out. Let me know, won't you?"

"I thought maybe you'd do something about it yourself."

"Not if I can get someone else to do my work for me." He meant me. I turned the doorknob and he said, "Is she dead?"

I turned to face him. "Who?"

"Mrs. Redstone."

"She's dead."

"You might be interested in Mr. Poupelle's last remark to me. Regarding his security. He said, as nearly as I can recall his peculiar idiom: 'After all, the old girl can't live forever.'"

He was enjoying himself, enjoying pushing that one at me. I said, "Interesting. She didn't live forever, at that, did she? Who does?" I went out.

16

Daphne smiled automatically when I came back into the reception room. I walked to the desk, leaned on it, and jerked my head toward Offie's office. "Bubbling over with joy, isn't he?"

"Who? Mr. Offenbrand?"

"No, of course not. The eight other guys in there." Her face went blank, so I went on quickly, "I was kidding. Yes, Mr. Offenbrand. Laughing Boy."

"Oh, he's not so bad."

"My lovely, you can do better." I grinned at her, all over my face, so she couldn't possibly mistake my meaning.

My jaws were starting to ache by the time she said, "Oh, yeah?" and lifted her left arm. "Look at that."

It was one hell of a bracelet. It sparkled like Times Square, squashed down into half a pound of metal and rocks. The rocks were diamonds. At least fifty of them circled a silver band, each diamond about the size of a peanut, and in the middle was something that looked like a cucumber.

"Oh," I said in a small, sick voice, "that."

She giggled. "And he *is* eighty-six. Maybe he'll remember me in his will."

"Honey," I said, "he isn't planning to die."

OK, so I was disgruntled. I left, hoping I had ruined everything for both of them. Maybe Offie wasn't planning to die, I thought, but if he didn't watch himself, that Daphne would kill him.

Outside I headed for the convertible, and almost the first thing I noticed was the gray coupé.

It had the same crumpled front fender; it was the same Ford that had made a pass at Three Eyes' hotel. It was parked in the next block on the opposite side of the street and facing this way. I couldn't see anybody in it, but there was a chance the driver was slumped almost out of sight. I went on to the Cadillac, climbed in, took the .38 from its holster, and put it on the seat beside me. I drove down Sunset toward the coupé traveling slowly and gauging the traffic so there'd be an opening when I got just past the Ford. Then I tramped on the accelerator, and as the Cad jumped forward, I pulled on the wheel, cut around in a U-turn, and skidded to a stop alongside the parked car. The gun was in my hand, and I was leaning on the right door of my Cad — as it stopped, but nothing happened. The buggy was empty. I got out, looked up and down the street and across it before I stuck the gun back in its holster. I didn't see anybody. A Yellow Cab half a block beyond Offenbrand's building pulled out from the curb and swung around the corner. Traffic streamed by, and several people stared at my oddly parked Cad.

I'd been tailed out here for sure. And whoever it was had played it pretty cagey. I looked into the Ford, but there was no registration slip on the steering-wheel post. I went over the car's inside, but there wasn't a thing in it; the buggy was clean. It had probably been stolen.

A police car stopped alongside. In it were a couple of boys I knew from the Hollywood Division and I told them the story. They said they'd check on the Ford and I left. This time I made sure I wasn't tailed by anybody — including Yellow Cabs. Back in downtown L.A. I parked in a lot, walked out the back way, and caught a cab myself. I had the driver take me around a few blocks and then down Hill Street to the Parker Building, where Paul Yates had once had his office.

I went up to the fourth floor, to the door lettered "Yates Detective Agency." Sergeant Billings was inside, seated in a swivel chair with his feet on the desk. He was a husky, good-looking young bachelor with six years in the department. He got up and stretched as I walked in.

"Hi, Shell. The Captain gave me a call, said you'd be in."

"How long you been on this kick, Bill?"

"Since they found Yates. Just sitting on things."

"Anything happen? Such as gorillas wandering in like clients?"

"Deader than Forest Lawn. No clients even. This Yates must've been taking life easy."

"He is now. That's why I'm here. I've got a big sympathetic spot in me for dead detectives." I pointed to a gray filing cabinet against the wall. "That all of it?"

"All the paper." He yawned. "You gonna be here very long?"

"Half hour anyway. Maybe more. Depends."

"I'll grab a fast hamburger."

"Grab a slow one. This will take me quite a while, I imagine."

He stretched again, then went out. I looked around the office. It was small, about eight by twelve feet, with a desk and swivel chair, two other wooden chairs, and a threadbare rug on the floor. Cigarette burns marred both sides of the desk. One of the windows was open and I looked down at Eighth Street and the little figures moving around four stories below. Then I went across the room to the files. There was only the single cabinet, but all four of its drawers were nearly full. Index tabs marked with the letters of the alphabet separated groups of paper-filled manila folders. I grabbed one at random, just to compare the style of the report with the one Yates had given Mrs. Redstone. It was dated '54, but the form was the same in most respects.

Under "R" I found a folder labeled "Redstone" and pulled it out. There were only the same three sheets I'd already seen, carbons of the report to Mrs. Redstone. There wasn't any substantiating data about Poupelle in the folder; but I hadn't expected any. Since Yates had apparently made all of that one up, there'd be no information to substantiate it, but one of the things I wanted to know was why he'd faked it.

There wasn't anything else about the Redstones in or near that folder. I looked, without luck, for the names Poupelle and Norman. And then I spotted a funny one.

I was squatting on my heels before the filing cabinet, flipping through the folders, just glancing at them, when a name caught my eye. At the same time I heard footsteps outside in the hall — Billings coming back with his hamburger. I didn't turn around. I fumbled through the papers to find that name again.

The footsteps outside came up to the door and I heard the knob turn. Then I had the paper in my hand. It was actually a sheaf of papers, two or three pages held together with a clip, with just "Client" written across the top.

The door opened and somebody came inside. I said, hardly aware of the words, "You'll get indigestion," looking for that name again. I found it — Fairview. I was excited, but through the excitement it occurred to me that Billings hadn't answered. The footsteps were coming toward me fast when I straightened my legs under me, started up, and tried to turn at the same time. I didn't make it. I didn't even come close to making it.

I got my head turned far enough so that I saw the guy, saw a blur of movement and one arm swinging fast toward my face. I tried to jerk my head away, but something crashed hard against my skull. My knees suddenly turned to water, and roaring pain ricocheted inside my head. I felt myself falling forward and grabbed at the legs before me, wrapped my fingers in cloth, and tried to pull. My head exploded into redness, and then into blackness.

Everything was moving. I couldn't see, but there was movement, and I could feel pressure underneath my armpits. Vaguely, through an ocean of pain, I remembered what had happened. I didn't know how long I'd been sapped; I didn't even know if I were in Yates's office anymore. But I knew I had to move, had to make my muscles and my eyes work.

There was that sickening swirl of movement again, and something hard pressed against my arm, then against my chest. The redness behind my eyelids grew brighter. Cooler air brushed over my face and dimly I heard the sounds of traffic below.

My mind cleared and suddenly I knew what was happening. My skin turned cold; my heart thudded. Yates's office was on the fourth floor of this building; whoever had slugged me had hauled me across the room to the open window I'd looked through earlier. And that shocked me into the first movement.

It was a small movement, not enough to make any difference, but at least I was coming out of it. I got one arm underneath me, pressed against the wall beneath the window, and forced my eyes partly open. I was looking down. Looking down the sheer side of a building, down four stories to the street below. Looking down a dizzy, frightening distance at blurred movement, and now there were hands on my ankles. He lifted, pulled both my feet off the floor. I heard him grunting and I tried to yell but I couldn't make a sound. I strained my right arm against the wall and tried passionately to kick with my heels.

I heard him swear filthily, surprise in his voice. Then I was spreading my arms, reaching back for the wall at either side of the window, kicking harder with my feet. I got my head turned away from that sickening vista below and caught a glimpse of the man as he wrapped both arms around my legs and squeezed them together.

There was sound at the other side of the room, something slammed into the door beyond him, and a voice cried out. The man holding me jerked his head around and I saw his face. One of his hands left my legs, slapped his chest, and moved outward again. I jerked my leg as a gun roared, but I was still looking at his face. One side of it seemed to leap away from his skull. His head snapped around as the gun boomed again and I felt the impact myself, jarring my flesh where he touched me.

Blood splashed against one of my hands, and then someone was pulling at me, jerking me back inside the room. It took me a while to get my eyes focused and air in my lungs. Sergeant Billings squatted in front of me, still hanging onto my coat with one of his big hands.

"Christ," I said. "Bill. Bill, I never . . ."

"Sit tight for a minute. That was a close one." He was sweating heavily. So was I.

Finally I got out a whole sentence. "I thought that was it. I thought I was going to fly four stories. Sweet Christ, Bill. What does a guy say? Thanks?"

"That's good enough. Can you tell me what happened?"

"Yeah." I was sitting on the floor inside that damned window. I said, "The bastard was going to air-mail me to Eighth Street. Man, it was touch and go there till you showed up. He touched me, and I was supposed to go. And I would have gone if you hadn't gulped that hamburger." I felt my head tenderly, wincing over two lumps.

I slid away from the window on my fanny, then managed to get to my feet. My knees felt a little as if they might bend the wrong way, but I was in reasonably good shape. Compared to what I might have been, I was in dandy shape. Then I saw the guy on the floor.

His face was pretty much unrecognizable now, but I knew it was Kid. I'd recognized him when I'd got that one clear glimpse of him, but it hadn't meant anything to me then. "Only name I know for him is Kid, but he'll be easy to run down. Part of the crowd that works for Norman."

My own words stopped me. I remembered the report I'd been looking at when the Kid had come in and walloped me. But Billings was saying, "He must not have expected anybody else to come in. And he'd probably have been alone in here if he hadn't stopped to burn something before taking, care of you."

"Burn something?"

"Yeah." He pointed to a heap of black ashes on the floor in the center of the room.

The worn carpet still smoldered and now I noticed the smell. I wondered how Kid had known so quickly the report was something that had to be destroyed.

I went to the swivel chair behind the desk, sat down, and lit a cigarette "Bill, I said thanks once, but let me — "

"Knock it off, Shell. You can shoot somebody for me next time."

"Name a couple. I'll get them today." He grinned and I asked him, "How did it look from your end?"

"I barged in and — you know what I saw. He had you half out the window. Tell the truth, I didn't know who had who out the window, but I pulled my gun and yelled. The guy jerked around and reached for his gun, and — well, I shot at him a couple of times."

"You didn't shoot at him, you shot in him. Thank my lucky stars. And your marksmanship."

He grinned. "You know what I was thinking? When I plugged him, I mean? I thought: If I hit him, he'll drop Scott out the window." He started laughing.

It seemed sort of funny and I started laughing with him and yelled, "So did I," and he shouted, "I hit him anyway!" and we whooped it up for a bit there. Long enough, at least, so that most of the strain left us both.

We were still yakking when I heard footsteps, in the hallway and Laurel came through the door.

She smiled a big relieved smile. "Shell. I was sort of worried. There's a whole gang of people down on the street pointing, up here and — ah — "

She'd just seen Kid. Her face got pale under the deep tan and for a couple of seconds I thought she was going to faint. I got her by the arm and turned her around and guided her out into the hall again.

In a minute she'd calmed down somewhat and said breathlessly, "Shell, what happened? That m-man — "

"Police officer shot him. He was in the act of breaking and entering. Breaking and entering my skull. Don't worry about him, he's a hoodlum. He was." I stopped. "What brought you here, honey?"

"I told you on the phone I couldn't stay at the house. I tried, but I couldn't, so I took one of the cars out of the garage and drove down. I wanted to see you. Shell, and you'd said you'd be here." Her face got a sort of green look again.

"Wait out here a shake," I told her, then went inside the office and closed the door.

Bill shook his head. "Who was *that?*"

"Laurel Redstone."

"Now, there's a beautiful hunk of woman . . . Redstone, did you say?"

"Yeah. The same." I grinned at him. "She's following me."

"Wish she was following me." He sighed. "Well, back to work."

While he put in a call to headquarters, I took a good look at Kid's body. The slug that had caught him in the face would have been enough; the second one had plowed into his chest. What was left of Kid's face, though, had a couple of deep scratches along the cheek. The knuckles of his right hand were skinned.

I looked up and said, "Bill, who you got on the phone?"

"Captain."

"Tell Sam the latest corpse is probably the guy who pushed Three Eyes. The coroner must have scraped some skin from under the little guy's nails by now." I pointed at Kid's cheek. "I imagine it came from there."

He nodded and relayed the info. I already could hear a siren in the street below whining to a stop. I turned back to Kid's body and an idea slapped my brain almost as hard as he had. I knew damned well I hadn't been tailed here. So how had Kid known where to find me?

I figured he'd been in that gray Ford at the Manor Hotel, then later near Offenbrand's suite of offices. I'd ducked him, then come here. I knew I'd ducked him and any other tail. And I hadn't told anybody I was coming to Yates's office except Sam. Then I remembered, there was another person I'd told.

There was Laurel.

17

Billings said, "What's the matter?"

He'd hung up and was looking at me curiously. I said, "I just thought of something."

"You look like you swallowed a fly."

I got to my feet, trying to think. After a moment I went into the hall again, and ran it down for the cops who were pouring down the hallway. They went on into the office and I walked over to Laurel, who was leaning against the wall.

"Honey," I said, "a funny thing just happened. That punk in there was tailing me earlier, then I shook him. But he showed up here right after I did. Almost as if he knew I'd be here. I didn't tell anybody I was coming here except the police and you. You didn't mention it to anyone, did you?"

She shook her head. "Of course not. I haven't even seen anybody. You know I wouldn't do anything like that."

"Yeah, I suppose so. But I can't figure how the guy knew I was here."

She looked at me hard out of those bright blue eyes. "Shell, you don't think I had anything to do with what happened, do you? Even accidentally?"

I hesitated only a moment, but that was too long. "No," I said. "I'll take your word for it, Laurel. It's just — "

"That's twice," she said flatly. "Twice you've made a remark like that, Shell. Once by the pool at Fairview, and now this." She was quiet, blue eyes narrowed and her face unsmiling. "All right, Shell." She turned and started walking away from me.

"Wait a minute, honey." I caught up with her and put my hand on her arm. She shrugged it off. "Shell, you don't trust anybody, do you? Not even me."

"Of course I trust you. Maybe you're about the only one in this mess I can —"

"Don't, Shell!" Her face was angry. She turned and walked away from me again, reached the head of the stairs.

"Where the hell are you going?" Crazy damn women, I was thinking. Stupid, sensitive damn women. "What in Christ's name's got into you?"

She glanced over her shoulder. "Don't yell at me, Mr. Scott. I'm going to Fairview." She paused, lips pressed tightly together. "And I don't want to know where you're going."

She started down the stairs, hurrying. Somebody behind me yelled, "Hey, Scott. C'mere a minute."

I started after Laurel and the guy called from the office, "Samson's on the phone, wants to talk to you."

Something was buzzing in my head, trying to get through to me. Something about Fairview and the guy that had taken the shot at me there. Laurel's words about my "suspicious" remark to her then had jogged something in my brain, but with the cop yelling at me it wouldn't fall into place. I looked around, then walked back to him.

"What's the matter with Sam?"

"Wants a word with you about this Three Eyes."

I got on the phone, listened a minute, and said, "It adds up, Sam. This Kid was one of the boys at the Afrodite. A gray coupé showed up at Three Eyes' Hotel, then near me on Sunset. I didn't see whoever was in it, but I'll bet it was Kid. Whoever killed Three Eyes had to knock him around first and got scratched up. Kid's got a couple of deep scratches on one cheek. It looks right, and the coroner can prove it."

"How'd Kid happen to show up and bang your thick head?"

"That's what bothers me, Sam. I talked to you about coming here, remember, but that's the only talking I did about it. Except for one person I called from my office, and I can't believe . . . "

I stopped and suddenly my skin was clammy. Two things slammed into my thoughts, then others. But over them all was the fear that Laurel would be killed if she went back to Fairview.

Sam was squawking into the phone but I didn't answer. I had to think. Billings said something but I shook my head. I squeezed my eyes shut and concentrated. Brown. That was the guy's name. Bob Brown, the guy prostrate after this morning's calisthenics at Fairview. And that call I'd made to Laurel . . .

I said rapidly into the phone, "Sam, get this quick. There's a bug on my office phone. Somebody's tapped it, so work fast if you can do anything at all."

"A bug? What makes you — "

"Somebody's been listening in on everything I've said over the telephone in my office. That's how Kid knew I was going to the Manor Hotel, and coming here later. He didn't have to tail me."

"We'll check, but you know how tough a job — "

I knew how tough a job it could be, and I didn't listen for the rest. Billings was beside me and I shoved the phone into his hand and ran out of the office, downstairs. Laurel was nowhere in sight; by this time she'd be well on her way, and angry, probably driving fast.

I raced to my Cad and swung into the traffic stream on Hill. It took me a hell of a time just to get to the end of the block and swing left to Broadway; then it got worse. I looked at my watch. It was one minute after five P.M. People were pouring out of offices, and cars clogged the streets. I was sweating by the time I reached Fourth Street, half a block from the Hamilton Building and my office.

The driver of an old Chevrolet up ahead was trying to push out from the curb and get into line. I kept my front bumper almost on the rear of the car ahead, determined that the Chevy wouldn't slow me down, but then I had an idea. I signaled for a stop and braked, leaving the man room to pull out.

He gave me a smile and a wave as he left the curb — and I swung into the parking space as he vacated it. I jumped from the Cad and headed straight across the street, stepping on one guy's bumper to get across. Despite honks and yells, I made it and ran toward the Hamilton Building.

In my office I grabbed the phone and dialed Fairview. I was sure that my phone had been tapped for the last couple of days, and that somebody would be listening right now. I had a little crossing up in mind.

I was pretty sure now that the guy who called himself Bob Brown had taken that shot at me and tried to kill Laurel before. I didn't think he'd make another attempt at Laurel now, what with all the pressure on him and on the brain behind him, but I wasn't taking any chances.

The receiver went up at the other end of the line. "Hello?" It was a man's voice.

"Who's speaking?"

"Mr. Blore."

I let out some breath. "This is Shell Scott. There's — "

"Where have you been, Scott? You get — "

"Shut up. There's a man named Bob Brown in camp. Get that — Bob Brown." I wasn't talking for Blore, but for that third party I hoped was listening to or recording this conversation. "He came into camp last month sometime, I don't remember just when."

"It was . . . let me see . . . "

"I don't care when it was." But the phone clattered; the ass must have thought I wanted the date. I yelled into the phone, but Blore was gone. In a couple of minutes he spoke again.

"Yes, on the fifteenth."

"That's not important. He's a plant, a killer."

Blore gasped. "What? You're not serious!"

"I'm serious as hell." He sputtered but I kept talking. "Where is he now?"

"Somewhere in camp, I'm not — "

"Find him. Stick with him. And get this, Blore. Don't tell him what I've just said. I'm coming out there. Just watch him. Understand? Don't say a word to him about this. And don't let him out of your sight."

"I can hardly — "

"You do it or I'll break your neck. Got that?"

He got it. "Ah, yes. Well, all right. I don't understand this."

"Just do it."

I hung up and flew out of the office. Traffic was still bad, but in fifteen minutes I was going out Figueroa. From there it took almost no time to reach Traverse Road, but as I swung left onto it I could see the clouds of dust already hanging in the air over it, starting about half a mile ahead. Starting at just about the place where the gate to Fairview was. Eight to five, Bob Brown had made that dust.

The wooden gate was wide open. I parked just inside it and trotted up the path into the clearing, ran across it to the main building. All around me activity was going on as usual. Man, these characters had a lot of energy — swimming, croquet, tag — but at least it all looked normal.

Mr. and Mrs. Blore were standing just outside the entrance to the Council Building. They both looked bewildered. I slid to a stop in front of them and said to Mr. Blore, "What happened after I called you?"

"I hung up and sat at the desk for a few moments, trying to understand what had occurred. Then I went outside to look for Mr. Brown." He smiled slightly. "I had no desire to have you break my neck."

"Sorry about that. There wasn't time to be nice. Please go on."

"Well, I'd barely got outside when the phone rang again. The only reason I answered was because I thought it might be you again. But it was another man. He asked for Bob Brown. Said it was important and to hurry."

"That fast, huh?" I said. He looked puzzled, and I added, "You know who phoned?"

"No. I have no idea. Well, I found Mr. Brown and his wife in their cabin."

"Where is it?"

He pointed. It was next to Laurel's on the right. "He went to the phone, talked a moment — I was right there beside him as you'd asked me to be — and then the odd thing happened. He dropped the phone, didn't even hang it up, and ran back to his cabin. Both he and his wife left immediately. Still running."

"She probably wasn't his wife. If he hadn't run, I might have killed the bum. And he knew it."

Mrs. Blore looked at me unhappily. "Mr. Scott, we've got to have some kind of explanation. What's going on? Earlier this morning there was a whole pack of reporters here. It was terrible. They asked the most awful questions. My husband wouldn't let them in, but he talked to them. And there's this newspaper story about Laurel — "

"Is she here yet?" I interrupted.

"She arrived just before the Browns left. I think she's in her cabin."

I broke away unceremoniously and tore for Laurel's little house. She was there, alive, very much alive, and she already had on the Fairview uniform. She was sitting in leaf-filtered sunlight, leaning back in a canvas chair in front of the cabin, and she didn't look angry, just confused.

"Shell," she said." What are you doing here? I thought — And do you know what just happened?"

"Yeah, I made it happen. You mean Brown?"

"Yes. He and Mary ran to their car and drove away. They weren't even dressed. They were carrying their clothes. What got into them?"

I sat on the ground at her feet and told her what had happened, including this last phone call to Fairview. I wound it up: "Whoever had the bug on my line could have been anywhere, in the Hamilton Building, in its basement, maybe blocks away. Or even miles away. He could have been the guy that called here right after me, or he might have relayed the info to whoever he was working for. Simple enough; say he relayed it, he could have picked up a phone and called anybody in L.A. — or South America — even while I was talking, and relayed the dope. Then the guy he phoned in turn put in a fast call to Brown here at Fairview and said, 'Fade out, the play is rumbled, blow because Scott's on his way to put the chill on you.' So Brown and his wife flew away like birds."

After a minute's silence, Laurel said, "How did you know it was Bob?"

"I wasn't sure — and, incidentally, Bob Brown isn't his name. Wish to hell I knew his real name. But this will kill you," I went on. "There were only three people really beat after my drawn-out calisthenics this morning. One of them was the health director, me. The other two were Bob and Mary Brown. We were apparently the only people here who couldn't take it." I grinned at her. "Maybe you've got something in this nauseating health kick of yours, after all. Hate to admit it."

I got the first small smile I'd had since she'd left the Parker Building. "There was another thing, too," I said. "You told me the babe's name was Mary."

"Yes. Bob and his wife, Mary. Or whoever she was."

"Yeah. Only the first thing he called her, when I walked over to them this early A.M., was Fran. He must have been pretty unstrung to call her by her right name — and that probably *is* her real name — but I was so unraveled at that point I didn't even notice."

"Then he must have shot at you yesterday?"

"Right. And tried to kill you before that. And whoever called him just a little while ago was responsible for both those items, and also either killed or knows who killed your mother. Ditto Paul Yates."

Her face clouded and she bit her lip. I kissed her lightly. "Sit right here, honey. I've got to make another call."

I ran all the way back to the Council Room. When I got there I was pretty well tuckered out. If ever this case ended, maybe I'd spend a few weeks at Fairview and get healthy. I called Homicide, got Samson.

"Sam, Shell." While I talked, Mr. and Mrs. Blore came inside and stood looking at me with their mouths hanging open. Right behind them came the dark, lovely little Peggy.

I told Sam, in fast sentences, about what I'd done and about Brown's taking off like a scalded ape. "So here's the crux: If you can find the guy on the tap — or Brown — you blow this thing wide open. Right now we can't know for sure who's behind the whole mess, but find out where that tap eventually wound up and it's cold. Because from there the call came in to Brown."

"I've got ten men looking all over hell-and-gone," Sam growled. "It's probably scrambled now, though."

"I know it. But there's a chance. And you might put out some teletypes on Brown." I described the guy, but from skin out Sam was on his own.

He said, "OK. Where you gonna be if I get word?"

"I'll call you. I'm going to be on my way in a minute."

After a little more talk we hung up and Mr. and Mrs. Blore descended on me at the same time. The gist of it was that they'd gladly flay me alive, but I explained a little and Mrs. Blore ran down. Her husband said, "Then you're really a detective?"

"That's right. I'm not Don Scott, but Shell Scott. And I'm a private investigator."

"So Laurel deceived us when she said — "

"No. I made her do it," I lied glibly. "It wasn't her fault. Don't forget you had a would-be murderer here in camp. Maybe a murderer in fact. Would you have preferred me and what I've done, or a bloody corpse or two here in Fairview?"

Mrs. Blore was looking at me. "What about tomorrow?" She practically wailed it.

"What do you mean, what about tomorrow?"

"The convention! For a year we've — "

Mr. and Mrs. Blore looked at each other and I was afraid they'd break down and blubber any minute. But Mr. Blore said, "Don't worry about it, dear. We'll work it out," and they left.

Peggy said thoughtfully, "So that's why you were so funny when you first came."

"Was I funny?"

"Odd, I mean. You acted strange. Not at all like what I expected."

"Well, you weren't what I expected."

She sighed. "You won't be here tomorrow, then?"

"Well, now," I said, "don't you go jumping to conclusions. Never can tell. One never knows, does one? I might be able to sneak in for a moment or so."

"If you're not here, everything will be all mixed up." She was smiling sadly.

"It'll be mixed up for sure if I'm here. But, ah, I'll do my best. Well, I've got to be on my way."

She turned sideways, leaving me enough room to get by. She really was cuter than the dickens. I thought of Laurel and looked at Peggy. Sometimes I hate myself. I went out, but as I went by Peggy I gave her a little pat on her behind. Don't get me wrong. I didn't grab it and yank it around or anything, just gave it a friendly cuff. Nothing crude, you know.

Then I swished out of the building and ran back to Laurel, wings on my feet. She was still sitting in the same place. And in the same way. She smiled at me this time.

"I've been thinking," she said. "You let him escape just because you were worried about me. You did it for me."

"Uh-huh. There wasn't any other way I could be sure that you'd be OK, honey. Doll. Sweet. I — "

"And to think I was angry with you."

"Not angry anymore?"

"Of course not."

She stretched slowly, hands curled again into little fists tucked under her ears, elbows pointing at the sky. Squatted precariously on my heels, I naturally lost my balance and toppled over. Toppled over forward. But then I shook my head vigorously and said, "I am leaving."

"Where you going?"

"Out. Away."

"Why?"

"I must. I've got a million things to do. A million. And if I stay here, that will leave nine hundred and ninety-nine thousand, nine — Oh, never mind." There was another reason for leaving. I hadn't been thinking too clearly outside of Fairview, but every moment here was bringing me closer to gibberish. I said, "Look, we've got to figure where you can go. Someplace safe."

"Can't I stay here? After what's happened, this should be safe enough, shouldn't it?"

I considered that and decided Laurel was thinking much more clearly than I was. Of course, I still had all my clothes on — but there I went, being vain and egotistical again. What she'd said was true enough, though, and the more I thought about it, the more sensible it seemed.

Finally I said, "I think you're right. That is, as long as I'm alive you ought to be safe here. As a matter of fact, this would probably be the safest spot for me, too, under the circumstances. It's highly doubtful that anybody will be bothered here now. Not after what's happened and the police being alerted and everything. Whoever we're after will know by now that the cops are up to date on Brown and Fairview. Stay here, then; just stay around other people."

"You're leaving?"

"I've got to."

"Will you be back?"

"Yeah, I've got to come back, too. And I'm going to need your help after a while. Tonight. I'm going to get that bullet, but you'll have to help me."

"Bullet? The one in the cliff?" I nodded and she said, "How in the world are you going to get up there?"

"I told you yesterday. I'm going to float up." I grinned at her and got to my feet. "I'll tell you about it later. In fact, I'll show you."

She shook her head, and I left.

It was after eight P.M. when I reached the Afrodite. The doors at the bottom of the steps were closed, but the neon sign was lighted and music blaring inside told me that the club was again open for business. I invaded the joint.

There was a five-piece combo at the rear of the small dance floor, playing the wildest, thumpiest, hottest Afro-Cuban music that had ever banged my eardrums inward. I liked it, but even more I liked the tall gal singing into a mike in the center of the dance floor. She was busty, all right, with a couple of maracas in her hands, and shaking everything like molasses in a Mixmaster. This, from Carlos's description, would be Juanita.

I walked closer to the dance floor, thinking this trip should be much more enjoyable than the last trip here. Then suddenly I reconsidered. At the opposite side of the floor from me, seated at a ringside table, was Babe Le Toot. There were two guys with her: a hood named Garlic and a hood named Young Egg Foo.

Maybe, I thought dismally, this trip isn't even necessary.

18

They spotted me at almost the same moment.

Foo leaned over the table and said something to Garlic, then they both leaned back and watched the show. Or pretended to. At least they weren't going to charge across the dance floor at me. Well, I was here, and I meant to stay. At least until I had a chat with Juanita. And maybe with Foo and his pal. The glass wall had been replaced and the birds were all calmed down again. It almost seemed a shame.

The only vacant seat I could see was the one at which a young red-haired guy sat alone, almost squarely in front of me, and directly across the floor from the two hoods and the hoodess. It was ringside, but I'd been spotted anyway, so I walked to the table, leaned down, and said, "OK, if I use that empty chair for a while?"

"Yeah, yeah," the redhead said. "Yeah. Take it anywhere."

His eyes were glued to Juanita and he didn't look at me, but it seemed he didn't quite understand. "I mean, right here, at your table."

"Yeah, yeah. Yow. Wow. Man, lookit that. Yeah."

At least I had a seat. I ordered a bourbon and water for me and another of the redhead's for him, then focused my attention on Juanita. Focusing on that babe was quite a trick. She was going in and out, and left and right, and up and down — all at once. She was singing, too. Carlos hadn't told me the half of it.

This Juanita was a sex cyclone with long black hair flying around every which way, a dark, full-lipped, sensual face, the lips writhing and twisting as she moaned words in some foreign language. The way she sang, she could have moaned in English and it would have sounded like a foreign language.

The rest of her looked as if approximately five feet ten inches of well-stacked woman had been mashed down into five feet seven inches, the excess bulging out and overflowing in enjoyable places. It was overflowing even more because of her frantic gyrations, in fairly good time to the clunks and whistles and toots from the men playing behind her. There were even some clunks and whistles and toots from the guys in front of her.

She was really moving, going all over the place, dragging the mike. The way some things were going, I thought they were going to keep on going, and I even imagined them flying through the air like that cockatoo. She was halfheartedly wearing a net brassiere, so flimsy it must have been made of piano wire to stay up there, a scarlet skirt that was open in front but swept around to touch the floor behind her, and something dark underneath the front of the red skirt. On her behind, which for a moment I thought was going to wind up in front, was a bunch of curving feathers in red and yellow and purple and black and white, all of them a rainbow blur right now. Except for high-heeled black pumps, the rest was Juanita.

She pulled at the red half-skirt, jerked it from her hips, and danced a little longer wearing only the shoes and bra, plus a gray G-string that looked as if it were made from the smoke of one cigarette. Then there was a wail from the band and the music stopped. Juanita stopped too.

All you could hear was the gnashing of teeth. Then applause boomed. Guys stamped their feet and whistled. Boors, I thought; clods. My hands began to hurt and I stopped. The guy at my table was going, "Yeah, wow, yeah," and I glanced across the room to see what my friends were doing.

They weren't doing anything. They weren't there.

At least, the two guys weren't. Babe sat alone at the table.

Involuntarily I ducked, thinking they would be behind me swinging saps, brass knuckles, tables, anything at my fat head. But nothing happened. Spotting my waiter nearby, I called him over. Had the two men gone someplace else? Yes, they had gone out the front door before Juanita finished her dance. He seemed surprised at that.

I was surprised too, but not for the same reason. I didn't suppose it actually made any difference, though. I was a bit disgruntled with myself for letting them creep out without my knowing it. But I'd never seen Juanita before. And a guy's got to have one or two little vices.

Right about then Juanita bowed and waved and blew kisses at everybody, then walked off stage toward an open door in the far wall. I could see part of a narrow hallway through it. I was just about to get up and follow her when I noticed the band members nudging each other and yakking back and forth. A couple of them looked at Babe Le Toot, who seemed to be in her cups. Or rather, in her highball.

Then the band started to play again. They didn't sneak into it, they hit it loud, wild, and gut-bucket — "St. Louis Blues" — and Babe's head snapped up as though somebody had yanked on her hair. A big, happy, all-gone smile spread over her chops and she leaped to her feet. While a trumpet went *waah-waah* she ankled out to the middle of the floor — and she seemed to have lost none of her technique. She had her blouse half off when the band stopped suddenly.

For a moment I got a kind of queasy feeling, thinking she must have tottered out half plastered and was going to be plenty embarrassed, but it wasn't at all like that. She did seem to sort of come out of a trance, and she looked around dazedly. Then she swung around to the band and laughed, ran to them and threw her arms around a couple of the guys and hugged them. They laughed it up and some of the men in the audience yelled, "You don't need music, Babe!"

I said to the young guy across the table from me, "What was that?"

For once he spoke intelligibly. "Guess you don't hang around here much. They pull that every other night or so when Babe's here. She gets outside a couple, and seems like the hooch plus 'St. Louie' makes her want to dance. Like she can't help it. They never let her go all the way, and she gets a boot out of it."

"So, I'd guess, do the customers."

"Yeah, man. Wish they'd let her go some night. She never has stopped while the music was playing." He grinned. "I'll be here if it ever happens."

"I'll bet you will. Thanks for the seat." I tossed off the last of my bourbon, got up, and walked to the doorway and into the hall. Light streamed into the hall from a doorway a couple of yards to my left, and when I walked over and looked inside, Juanita was sitting in a chair before a dressing table, putting on some more lipstick. She should have put on more than lipstick.

Her back was to me but she could see me in the dressing-table mirror. I said, "Hi," and she raised her eyes to meet mine in the mirror.

"Who're you?"

"OK if I come inside?"

"I guess. Who are you, anyway?"

I went in and shut the door, took out my wallet and showed her the photostat of my license. "Like to talk to you a little."

"Another cop," she said. "Three of them already talked to me." She swung around on her chair to face me. "Say, you know Carlos Something-or-other? Lieutenant, I think. He was nice."

She had no accent at all, but she looked Latin, and Carlos was Cuban, besides being a good-looking cat and one hell of a rumba artist. "Sure," I said. "Carlos Renata. Buddy of mine."

"Sit down." She pointed to a chair so spindly that I didn't think it would hold me, but it did, and I said, just to soften her up a little more, "Really enjoyed your act, Juanita. First time I've caught it. Not the last, though. You've got a beautiful voice, you know."

She beamed. She must have heard about that body and dance of hers a thousand times, but this was music to her ears. Actually, her voice stank. But if three cops had already talked to her without learning much of anything, three cops including Carlos, I had to get on her good side somehow. Not that she had a bad side.

She said, "Do you really mean it?"

"What do you think, Juanita?"

"I think you're a pleasant liar." She was smiling.

I grinned at her "Well, I had to say something."

"I can't sing for sour apples, and I know it. But it sure sounded good." She laughed.

"You should worry. Kirsten Flagstad doesn't dance so good, either."

We yakked like that for a couple of minutes, and got along famously. When I asked her about Yates and the rest of it, she didn't give me any trouble. The outfit she was wearing gave me a little trouble, but I listened closely. There wasn't anything I hadn't got from Carlos or Sam: Yates had been here Saturday night, the night he'd been killed. A little after midnight he'd been called to the phone, left, and that was it. In the club that night had been Babe, Foo, Strikes, and a guy she called Sardine Lambert. It was a new name, at least, so I asked her about it.

"He's another of the bunch that work out at the castle. You know where it is?"

I nodded. "I've been there. As a matter of fact, that's my next stop tonight."

"Then you've seen that goofy knight they've got out there. Two men dress up and parade around. One of them's Lambert."

"Which, I suppose, is why they call him Sardine. Another of Norman's boys, huh?"

"Works for him."

"How about a guy named Bender? Brad Bender."

Her lips parted and her eyes opened wider, but quickly her features went back to normal. It seemed funny, so I pushed it around gently.

"Seems like I heard his name somewhere. He one of the bunch that hung around here with Foo and Strikes?"

She didn't say anything, so temporarily I shifted the subject. "How about Andon Poupelle? Was he here the night Yates got that call?"

"I don't think so. He's been here a few times. Not lately, though. I didn't know who he was until Carlos described him."

I went on casually, "About Brad Bender. Didn't Carlos or one of the others ask you about him?"

"No."

I remembered then that I'd given Bender's name to Sam only yesterday; the police had talked to Juanita a day or two before. "Well, hell," I said, "you know the guy, don't you?"

"I know him. Why? What's the matter? I . . . go out with him quite a bit."

"Go out with him? When was the last time?"

"Over a month ago. What's all this about? He isn't in any trouble, is he?"

"That's the point. Nobody's heard anything of him for about a month. I understand he used to hang out here, and then, bang, he's not here any more. Word is, maybe he got hurt. Hurt bad. Maybe fatally."

I was watching her while I spoke and her lips parted again. "Oh, no," she said quietly. "He said he'd see me again in a month or so."

"When was this?"

"About that long ago. A month, I mean. Maybe less."

"You two . . . have an understanding or something?"

"No, he's just a nice guy, is all. Can you tell me any more? I mean, is there a chance he . . . isn't hurt?"

"There's a chance. You say you saw him about a month ago?"

"Not quite that long. I can find out in a minute. Only I didn't see him, he phoned me from Vegas and said — "

"From where? Las Vegas, Nevada?"

"Yes."

I got up and lit a cigarette, then sat down again. "Baby, find out when that call was. Find out for sure. And what did he say to you?"

She went to her dressing table and opened a drawer, pulled out a small calendar. "I marked the day he called," Juanita said, "so I could figure about when I might see him again." She turned around with the little calendar in her hand and added, "It was sort of funny. He wouldn't tell me why, just said he had to stay out of town for a month or so. I wasn't supposed to mention it to anybody. But if he's hurt . . . "

She turned back a page on the calendar and ran her finger over the sheet. "Here it is. He phoned me on June 10. I hadn't seen him for over a week then."

That was about all of the conversation. I stayed a few minutes more, then got up again. "Don't worry too much about Bender, Juanita," I said. "I think maybe I shook you up for nothing. I think your boyfriend's all right."

"I hope so."

"You know what? I kind of hope so too."

She gave me a big smile as I left, but I hadn't said that to please her.

In the main part of the club I looked around, but my husky chums weren't in sight. Even Babe was gone now. I headed for Castle Norman.

Heading there was one thing; getting in was another. My first visit with Ed Norman had convinced me that dire things would happen to me if I were foolish enough to go back. And the way things were shaping up, I had a hunch Norman might shoot me on sight. But there was a vague idea dangling from one convolution of my brain.

If I could ever get inside the castle without being recognized, I might make a little progress tonight. But it would take some doing, and I'd need some help. I would need some help from Sardine Lambert.

19

Castle Norman was brilliantly lighted, and when I'd parked in the lot and walked a little way toward the drawbridge and entrance, I could see that silly knight sitting on his horse.

I didn't want him to see me, however, so I walked to my left onto the green lawn fronting the castle. Out a few feet from the edge of the moat was a big bush that would hide me from Sardine while I watched the guy for a while to see what his actions were. In case I had to duplicate them.

A man and woman arrived, then another couple, but Sardine didn't do anything fancy, just sat at the rear of the drawbridge, his lance pointing toward the sky, a red cloth dangling from the end of it, the color matching a red plume sticking up from his helmet.

I'd seen enough. I waited until he was looking away from me, then walked to the moat and into it. The water was only about three feet deep, but wet, and the goo on the bottom was sticky as glue. I walked along the side of the moat next to the wall around Castle Norman, and from here I couldn't even see Sardine — or whoever was in that armor.

I checked my holster, to be sure the Colt Special was handy, then bent over and walked to the drawbridge and crouched under it, waiting for a moment when Sardine's back would be turned to me. A car pulled into the parking lot, lights flicking over me, and I ducked a little lower. It was sure sloppy. In a couple of minutes four people walked from the car and into the castle, laughing and making cracks about Sir Lancelot as they passed the mounted knight.

Sir Sardine looked after them as they went out of sight, turning his horse around — and his back to me. I straightened up, grabbed the wooden drawbridge's edge in my hands, and hauled myself onto it as silently as I could.

No one seemed to be in the small courtyard, and I hoped to hell nobody else showed up for a few minutes.

I straightened up, took two steps toward Sardine — and he heard and jerked his head around. He recognized me, all right, and started to yell, but he only half finished yelling because when his head had started to turn I'd started running toward him.

Sound came out of his throat as I jumped at him. One of his gauntleted hands came up as I crashed into him and his horse, but I grabbed his arm and jerked as I slid down. He tried to bring his other fist around to slug me, dropping the long lance, but he was on his way down by that time. He landed with one hell of a crash on the wooden flooring beneath us and for a second I thought he was going clear on through. He didn't move after he landed. He was breathing, but he was out cold. The horse shied away, snorting.

I bent over and grabbed Sardine beneath the shoulders and hauled him over to the big bush on the lawn where I'd hidden for those few minutes. It took a while to figure out the combination, get the armor off Sardine, then bind and gag him, but I managed it. Hunks of metal were laid out before me like pieces of a three-dimensional jigsaw puzzle, but I'd noted how the armor came off and thought I could get it onto me. Sardine was about my size. This stuff was not authentic Golden Age armor; some of it tied on, some of it just slipped on, and a couple of items were equipped with canvas and zippers, probably so that Sardine could dress himself. I started struggling with it.

Finally I was in. I knew I had on a helmet, a gorget, and gauntlets, plus roweled spurs for my feet, on my own shoes, but the rest of it I had probably never heard of. The part over my chest and back was in one solid piece that I'd had to wriggle into like a stiff girdle. The helmet's visor moved up and down, and when it was down I couldn't see too well, looking out through vertical slits, but at least nobody could look in at me, either. There were metal shin and thigh guards, plus some other doodads. I started creaking back toward the drawbridge. The white horse didn't seem leery of me now that I was suitably attired, and stood quietly as I walked toward him.

Two more cars ripped into the parking lot. People piled out and came noisily in my direction. Like the previous couples, they got a big kick out of the knight and started yelling at me. The main doors of the castle opened and somebody looked out, then trotted toward me. It was the husky boy I'd had the beef with my first time here.

I got ready to slug him if I had to, but he stopped a yard from me and said, "What's the matter with you? Why ain't you on your horse, Sardine?"

I unwound my fist. The laughing group was alongside us by now, and they stopped, watching us. I was sweating more than the armor's warmth could account for, but I said, "Dropped my lance."

I didn't even know what Sardine's voice sounded like, but my tones were suitably muffled by the helmet — and the customers had hysterics.

"Dropped his lance!" one yelled. "Caught him with his lance down!" Husky allowed himself to laugh with them. There was more laughter while I climbed onto the horse, since the damned armor seemed to weigh a ton — besides which, I'm not accustomed to climbing onto horses. I know nothing at all about plenty of things, but especially horses.

Husky handed me the lance, then talked it up with the customers and herded them toward the castle. But he swiveled his head around and gave me a very dirty look.

I allowed them a couple of minutes to get inside, and used the time to calm myself. Then I got off the horse and leaned the lance against the arched entranceway. I knew that if I just walked confidently inside the castle and through the rooms to Norman's office, I might make it easily. The main thing was to act normal.

I pushed off. I walked straight to the castle and inside as the other armored knight on duty opened the door for me. He said something but I ignored him. A few guests looked at me casually, but knights in armor were old hat to them now and they glanced away. I walked over to the red-draped entrance to the game room. Husky stood beside it and started to say something, but I shook my head back and forth, pointing at the door.

I kept walking straight at it, as though there weren't the slightest possibility that he wouldn't open it, and I clumped by him into the game room. The damned armor was getting pretty heavy, and I wondered if it might not be tougher to get outside than it was to get inside.

At first I didn't see anybody that I recognized in the game room. Then I saw Ed Norman. He was wearing a tux, talking to a man and a woman, and his back was to me. I kept going as casually as I could across the room to the metal door, kicked it gently with my foot.

As the bolt slid back inside I glanced around with a creak. Norman still hadn't noticed me. When I turned back to the door it was half open, and before me stood the Mental Monster. We stared at each other: Metal Monster meets Mental Monster.

"Haw?" he said.
"Yuh," I said.
"Sardine?"
"Yuh."

I walked at him like a tank and he stepped aside. So far it had been almost too easy, and I was wondering when my luck and confident air — and maybe blood — would run out. But I wasn't much worried about this character.

He closed the door behind me. I coughed and growled, "Boss sent me for something."

He slid the bolt home and I clumped to Norman's office. The door wasn't locked and I went inside, shut the door behind me, and sprang into action. Yeah, I could about spring an inch off the floor in this outfit. But I made it to Norman's desk, took off my gauntlets, and started tugging at the drawers. Only the middle desk drawer was locked.

The desk was wood, and not hard to break open. I kicked out the bottom of the drawer, then pawed through the papers that fell to the floor. I found one thing I wanted. Clipped together were three sheets of typed paper: Yates's report to "Client." Under the clip behind the last page were six photographs, unmistakably of Laurel, and apparently taken at Fairview.

It was a tight squeeze, but I managed to stuff the whole batch under my metal breastplate. None of the other papers looked interesting, though I leafed through them quickly. I stood up, my stomach muscles knotted with tension; I could feel the tightness at the base of my skull and in my neck. It was all I could do to keep from dashing for the door, but I made myself go over to that chair I'd noticed in the corner the night before and knelt down. The stained area had been cleaned, all right, but I felt pretty sure that there'd still be traces of blood in the cloth and nap. I pulled at the carpet with my fingernails, got a little pile of the nap in my right hand. There wasn't any way to get it into my pocket, so I stuffed it down inside one of my socks. That was it. It was time I got the hell out of here.

It was past time.

I was kneeling on the floor, pulling my gauntlets back on, when the door opened behind me. Somebody said, "What in Christ's name are you doing?"

It was Norman. My back was to him, but I recognized his voice. And there were a couple of other voices. I got up slowly and as I turned to face the doorway I took one step toward it. Norman stood just inside the room, staring at me, a frown on his thick, scarred face. On his right was Husky, and beyond them in the hallway, peering past them, was The Brain.

I took another step forward and said, "Somebody busted in here Lookit the desk."

Norman didn't cooperate. He kept looking at me, his frown deepening. The sound of my voice had puzzled him, and suddenly he said, "You — " and his right hand slapped down and behind him to his hip. It came up with a snub-nosed gun, but by that time I'd taken my third step and was swinging my right fist, plus a couple of pounds of metal, up at his chin.

Husky yelled something and started toward me as my fist landed with a horrible crack on Norman's chin. His head snapped back and he spun sideways and fell soundlessly to the carpet. I went down a little way with him, just about as far as Husky's middle, then pivoted toward him and my left fist sank in, and in, and in. He made a great whistling sound and bent over with his arms sticking out ahead of him. He fell, groaning horribly, and as I straightened up, The Brain came jumping toward me.

I raised both hands and he stopped jumping and actually backed away. That perplexed expression spread over his craggy face again — and this time he had good reason to be perplexed. I realized then that I had quite an advantage. The only way any of these guys could slug me was at the risk of breaking their hands clear up to their ears.

Brainy drew back a great big right fist, his face a montage of flickering emotions. Then his mouth dropped open, way open, and he just stood there, gawping at my gleaming armor.

All that took only a second or two, and just as he said, "What the crud — " I raised one metal-covered fist over his head like a hammer. He actually lifted his eyes to it, sheer hopelessness in his expression. And then, *splat*, I hammered him good on the forehead. His face got a peaceful look and his eyes flickered partly shut and tried to merge. I had finally met someone looking himself in the eye. He was gone away from here before he hit the floor.

I jumped over him. That is, I meant to jump over him, but I just clanked and landed on him. Then I clumped to the door, slid the bolt back, and hightailed it for the game room. Things looked normal in here, and I began to think maybe I'd make it out. But then the reaction from what I'd gone through started to catch up with me. Sweat covered my body and I could feel a thumping pulse in the hollow of my throat, and at my temples. I clumped through the game room, out through its now-unguarded door, and headed for the exit. I felt as if I were carrying a mountain on my back.

I almost made it. I was ten feet from the door when a hoarse, weak shout rang out behind me. "Stop him! It ain't Sardine!"

I glanced around to see Husky hanging to the open door, a hand pressed to his stomach. Then he fell — and when I turned my head back a brother knight was coming toward me. This was different from the last brawl; we were starting out on even terms. But I guess I was so accustomed to slugging guys and having them go all loose that I thought the same thing would happen this time. Sometimes a confident air isn't enough.

I hauled off and slammed a hard right to his chin and crossed with a chopping left to the breadbasket: *Clang-clang!* He didn't go loose, but my knuckles felt as if they'd spread about eight feet. The knight staggered a little, then swung back gamely and slugged me a couple of times. He had no more sense than I did.

There was one hell of a lot of noise, guys yelling and women screaming, but ringing loud and clear over everything else was the clamor of battle. All we needed was a band playing the "Anvil Chorus." We sounded like two streetcars at the same crossing.

Old Ironsides had his right fist drawn back, and when he launched it at me I jerked my head aside. As it whistled by me I reached out with my left hand, pushed up his visor, and hauled my right fist around in an arc that ended on his chops. It damn near ended his chops. Teeth went every which way and the only clang this time was when he landed flat on the floor.

Boy, *everybody* was screaming. I glanced over my shoulder as I went at a staggering half trot out the door into the courtyard. People were spinning around; Husky had fallen by the far door, apparently passed out. I made it to the drawbridge and the white horse — and then really I started to quake in every limb.

Two guys were walking this way from the parking lot and under the bright lights I could see their faces well enough, but I just didn't believe it. It simply couldn't be Garlic and Young Egg Foo, not after what I'd been through.

But it was true; even though my vision was hampered by the visor, I could see the two hoods. They were just strolling casually this way, though, and obviously they knew nothing about what was going on inside the castle.

I grabbed the lance leaning in the archway as I passed, struggled up onto the horse, and said softly, "Come on, horse. Move. Giddap."

I was hoping a lot of things: that Husky would stay unconscious and that nobody else would figure out what had happened until I'd reached the Cad; that Foo and Garlic would think I was Sardine; that this horse would move and that I would wake up from this bloody nightmare. The horse stayed motionless.

And then everything fell apart. There was noise, yelling, and I saw Foo racing toward the bush where I'd left Sardine. The bum must have come to and worked the gag out of his mouth.

Everything happened like a movie run at double speed. *Zip,* and Foo was at the bush; almost instantaneously he was racing away from the bush and at me, roaring like a bull elephant. Garlic trumpeted and raced at me too. I had got myself into a pickle.

There was a gleam of light in Garlic's hand. It was a gun. Garlic was going to shoot me. Well, by God, I'd give *these* guys a battle, too. I reached for my gun — *clang*. "Oh, Lord," I moaned. It's a hell of a note when a guy has to take off his pants to get at his banger. A quick draw in this outfit would take approximately fifteen minutes.

Well, maybe I couldn't get at my gun, but I had a lance and a horse. I'd lance them, I'd run them through, I'd string them up like beads. I lowered my lance and charged.

Yeah, charged. I don't know beans about horses. I leaned forward shouting, "Cck, cck, go, Bossie!" but nothing happened except that the hoods got much closer. Then I raised my legs and banged them down again, and that stupid horse finally went into action. He leaped forward with a whinny, and hoofs drummed over the drawbridge.

I aimed my lance. Garlic was faster than Foo, and consequently a few yards ahead of him, on my left. He seemed sort of startled to see me bearing down on him, lance pointing at his nose. But he flipped his gun and fired, the bullet swishing past my helmet; then my lance caught him on the forehead and spun him back and around like a top. The lance flew from my hand as I jerked my head the other way, to my right toward Foo.

I was practically on top of Foo, just a couple of yards away, so automatically I leaped for him, lunging forward from my horse. Only again I forgot about all this armor.

Anyway I was aimed right, and both my gauntleted hands caught him hard in the middle of his horrified expression, but only then did I start thinking about what would happen to me. And then it was too late.

I went sailing past him, and through the slits in my visor I could see the ground leaping up at me. My hands were outstretched, rigid, but I was just too heavy when I landed. First I felt my arms buckling. Then I felt my head buckling.

And then there was a sound like the pearly gates swinging together, and a squishing, and a rainbow-streaked blackness. Something new had been addled.

20

Consciousness returned, but I was only half out of the blackness while trying to get to my feet. I got my legs under me, but they wobbled. I staggered a few steps forward and tottered around. It was all very strange, eerie, unnerving. I seemed to be in a jail of some kind. I could see the bars right in front of my eyes. Off in the haziness ahead of me was a castle. I had been thrown back through time to the days of chivalry, to King Arthur's court. The chivalrous bastards had put me in a dungeon and had been beating me about the head with battleaxes. I had to escape. If only I could clear my head, I thought. I took another step — and fell down.

Cold wetness crawled all over me. In a few seconds my head was clear. The cold water had shocked me back to consciousness and suddenly I knew what had happened. Those bastards had flooded the dungeon!

They were drowning me. Chivalry — hah! Then suddenly I realized I had fallen into the moat. I felt as if I were sinking down, down through ooze, and it hardly seemed worthwhile to try to get up. Even if I did, somebody would ventilate my head some more. But I did get up, slopped hip-deep to the moat's edge, and climbed out like the Beast from One Fathom.

I was still dazed, and my head hurt enormously, but I guessed that it couldn't have been much more than a minute or so since I'd fled the castle, because nobody was rushing out after me yet. Garlic was moving a little, about ten yards away. Near my feet, Foo was sprawled, motionless. Close to him was a .45 automatic.

There was noise from the front of the castle and I heard somebody shouting. I scooped up the automatic and worked its slide, cocking the hammer. Two men ran onto the drawbridge and stopped when they saw me. One of them yanked up a gun and fired. I slammed two shots at them and they turned and ran like hell out of sight.

I started toward the parking lot. I'd taken about three steps when there was another gunshot; the slug zipped by me, actually pinging against the top edge of my shoulder armor. I swung around and dropped to my knees as the gun — in Garlic's hand — blasted again. He was prone, arm extended toward me, and I pulled the .45 toward him, squeezed the trigger three times, and saw his body jerk violently, then roll completely over.

I ran for the Cad, crawled under the wheel, and started the engine. Then I hoisted the .45 over the windshield and emptied it at the archway, just in case somebody got an idea about trying to follow me. I threw the gun away, slammed the Cad into gear, and took off. More gay partygoers had arrived while I was emptying the gun. As I drove away, they stared at me. They really stared.

Nobody followed me, or, if anyone did, he didn't get close. In half an hour I was at Jay's surplus yard, "Anything for a Price." The stained, and now wet, nap from Norman's carpet was in an envelope in the glove compartment of my car, along with the Yates report and photographs. And I was out of my armor.

Jay had the stuff I'd ordered ready for me. I saw it right away. Couldn't miss it, for that matter.

Three heavy ropes went straight up into the air like a triple Indian rope trick, their lower ends anchored by big hunks of lead, the top ends held up in the air by large gas-inflated balloons. I already had the top down on the convertible, so by lifting the hundred-pound lead chunks and carrying them to the car, then dropping them behind the seat, I was ready to go in little more than two minutes. The hundred-pound lead pieces, with the balloons tugging them upward, seemed to weigh only about twenty pounds apiece.

Jay put the Coleman lantern, shovel, rope ladder, coil of piano wire, and a hunting knife into the car and I wrote out a check for him, using one of his dry blanks. It was for a disgusting amount of money, but I'd expected that. I'd get most of it back, anyway, when I returned the stuff.

When I was in the car and ready to go, Jay looked at me warily. "What you gonna do with all this junk? This a new way to move hunks of heavy stuff?"

"No. But that's an idea I'll add to my list, Jay. This thing has endless possibilities. Why, you could attach a couple of bundles of these balloons to guys working on skyscrapers or bridges, and if they fell off they'd just float down. This thing may do away with elevators."

He stuck out his chin at me. "Come on. I knocked myself out getting the stuff and filling the damned balloons for you, so give. Incidentally, they're filled with natural gas, so don't light any cigarettes around them. Blow yourself up, maybe. Come on, boy, level with me."

I told him the truth, but I think he still felt I was holding out on him. "I am," I said, "going to hang a ladder in the sky. And I'm going to climb up the ladder and dig a bullet out of a cliff."

He was still laughing, sort of wildly, when I drove off. I drove very slowly and carefully, making sure I passed under no electric wires or overhanging tree limbs. And also because my head hurt like the devil. At Fairview I parked in the lot and went to Laurel's cabin. She wasn't there, but I found her in my cabin again. After a touching reunion she drew back from me and I stopped touching her.

She said, "Ugh. Shell, you're all wet. How did it happen?"

"I fought a sick dragon. He kept belching at me. I'm a knight, come to sweep you — "

"What in the world are you talking about?"

I didn't tell her. I wasn't ever going to tell anybody. Instead I said, "Honey, want to help me in a little operation I've got planned?"

She smiled wickedly. "Uh-huh."

"I refer to the operation I mentioned this afternoon. Getting that bullet. This afternoon it seemed important — in fact, it *is* important — but now everything is dreamlike."

It was, in a way. My mangled head kept throbbing and, occasionally, pink and blue lights flashed in my eyes. Wouldn't it be a scream, I thought, if I were off my rocker?

Laurel said, "All right. What is it that you want me to do?"

I told her. She told me I was mad. I told her I wasn't. After a bit of that she said, "Can you really do it?"

"Of course. I've got it all figured out. Cost me a fortune, but it'll be simple. If I don't fall and break my neck. But nothing can happen to me tonight. This is my charmed night. This night is magic." Those pink and blue lights flashed again.

We left. I drove the Cad as close as possible to the pool where I'd been shot at, then we lugged all the equipment up to the edge of the cliff. With a sledgehammer I drove a long, curved bar, like an overgrown staple, deep into the ground. Then I fastened one end of a thick rope to it. In fifteen minutes the setup was ready.

Laurel looked at me in the light of the burning Coleman lantern. Then she looked up at the spot where the balloons were, invisible in the blackness above us. Using the piano wire and rope, I'd tied all three bunches of balloons together so that their combined lifting power was about 250 pounds, more than enough, with the lead weights now removed, to support me and several extra pounds besides. The rope holding them was fastened to the curved bar in the ground, and tied to it and hanging down to the ground was the rope ladder. Now I could climb up into the sky.

Laurel said, "There's only one thing wrong. Seriously, it makes some sense now that I see it, only your ladder goes straight up. It's high enough and close to the cliff, but you said you've got to dig way out there on the right, over the water."

"That's where you come in, honey. I'll climb part way up and tie this line" — I showed her the small rope in my hand — "to the thick line the balloons are tied to. You take the other end and walk around to the far side of the pool. While I'm on the ladder, you pull until I tell you to stop. You pull me out over the water, and I climb up or down the ladder till I'm where I want to be. Simple?"

"I guess. Or else you're simple."

"Young woman, this is sheer genius. The balloons will pull straight up; you pull toward you. I'm right there at one point of the triangle, happy as can be. It has something to do with geometry. Or is it algebra?"

"OK, Einstein. Let's see you operate."

I went up the ladder, carrying the Coleman lantern and a shovel. By that time Laurel was at the opposite side of the pool. Soon, with her pulling gently, I was exactly where I wanted to be. I wired the lantern to one rung of the rope ladder over my head, then started scraping at the earth side of the cliff with my little shovel.

Getting the slug itself was nothing after all the preparation; in fact, it was anticlimactic. When I'd first got into position I could see the day-old bullet hole in the cliff, and it was just a matter of scraping at it till I got in deep enough. I'd sway out from the cliff occasionally, or get out of position because those balloons weren't rigid up there, but there wasn't much to this part of the operation.

"Tell you what, Laurel," I said while I dug. "We might use this idea in the Long Beach Pike. Fix up a spot in the amusement zone like the surface of the moon, strap balloons on people so they're light, and they can jump around like crickets."

"Swell," she said. "We'll give them membership cards, enlisting them as moon people. You get the first membership. You know why nuts are called lunatics, don't you, Shell?"

"Yeah. But — woops. Wait a shake, baby." I'd dug deep enough. I could see the dull gleam of the slug and in another minute I had it in my hand. The point had expanded and folded back on the jacket like a beat-up metal mushroom, but the ballistics boys downtown wouldn't have any trouble identifying it and comparing the marks on its barrel with another bullet. And I had little doubt that they'd identify this one as a Silvertip .30-.30 slug. I went down to earth again.

Laurel trotted around the pool, her body a pale glow in the darkness, getting more substantial — and prettier — as she got closer. She ran up and stopped before me, smiling slightly. Then she sobered and, in mock surprise, said, "Where in the world did you come from?"

"From there," I said solemnly, pointing up. "My God!"

"Not at all. I am Eekle from there." I pointed up. "I claim this joint in the name of Arcturus. I have traveled many light years. I have very light vehicle. I claim you in the name of Eekle. Argle zoop slangslop."

"What's this argle something?"

"Language Arcturus. My language. I bright as hell, speak all kinds slop."

"Oh, argle yourself. Let's go back to the cabin."

"I've got to get this slug downtown." I grinned. "But after that I'll be back, and I mean to framblot you."

"What's that?"

"Old Arcturian custom. Come on, let's go."

We went. I just left the stuff there, balloons and all. Tomorrow the nudists were going to be surprised when they saw it. At least, that's what I thought then. If I had known the truth, I'd have slashed my wrists.

21

At the central station I gave the bullet to the boys in SID and they started checking. I left the envelope containing the bits of Norman's carpet with them, too, then drove to City Hall.

I talked to the detectives on the night watch in Homicide, phoned Samson, woke him up, and jawed awhile. I told him all I knew and suspected about Bender. Also what I'd guessed so far about Ed Norman, Andon Poupelle, Vera, and the collection of hoods. Samson got dressed and came downtown.

We were still drinking coffee in his office when he said, "OK, Shell, I want you to sit tight, don't make a move from here on in unless you get word from me."

"But, Sam, I've got a couple — "

"Listen to me." He looked at a bunch of papers spread over the top of his desk. "One, that paraffin test on Mrs. Redstone was positive; she fired a gun. But this wouldn't have been the first time a killer wrapped a stiff's finger around a trigger and let go a second shot, and two empty cartridges were in that little .32 of hers. So we had the crime-lab engineer make up a scale drawing of the room and windows. Only one window was open. An imaginary line from the chair Mrs. Redstone was in, passing out that window, went right to a couple of trees. The slug was in the base of one of them."

"The second slug. That pretty well kicks out any idea of suicide. All the more reason why I should — "

"Wait a minute. Until a little while ago the newspapers were taking it easy on us, figuring it probably was a suicide. But they know different now, and if Mrs. Redstone as a suicide was front-page news, Mrs. Redstone murdered is a whole circus. All hell is about to bust loose. First thing in the morning." He paused. "Mrs. Redstone's killer naturally hoped, and undoubtedly expected, that the kill would stay a suicide — that nobody would be looking for a murderer. If it hadn't been for you, Shell, I think that's the way it would have been. But he'll soon know positively, if he doesn't already, that he's in plenty of hot water. He'll have to make a move, one way or another, in a very short time."

"Uh-huh." I thought of something. "Nobody's told me yet, Sam. How about Kid? Did the coroner check — "

"Right. Skin and blood from Three Eyes' face was under Kid's nails. I said this one's hot, but it's going to get hotter. Everybody from the Mayor down through the Commissioner is jumping up and down on the Chief, and he may eat me alive as it is. We haven't been able to locate Poupelle and his wife since they were down here that one time. Looks like they've skipped. Until we know more, you'd better sit tight. We mess this one up, I'm dead."

We were quiet for a little while. I'd given Sam the report I'd filched from Norman's office. Two things in it had been of interest to me. First, it was dated June 14; and secondly, it proved that Yates had discovered Laurel's presence at Fairview. Yates had put a tap on Mrs. Redstone's phone and heard a conversation between her and "Sydney" at Fairview, whereupon he'd gone to a spot near there and snapped some pix using a telephoto lens on his camera. It was also rather interesting that the report to "Client" was dated one day *before* Yates's report to Mrs. Redstone, which report had played up Poupelle as God's gift to angels.

Sam's phone rang. He talked to somebody for a while, said, "You haven't got anything on that carpet fuzz yet? OK, let me know as soon as you do. Yeah, I'll be here all night." He hung up and looked at me. "Well, there's your slug. Identical with the one that killed Yates. From the same rifle."

"Bob Brown. That helps."

"Helps plenty. Only we haven't got Brown. Whoever he is."

"Norman's in this."

"All the more reason to make damned sure before we move. Shell, don't barge around and mess anything up until we've got a tight case."

"If you find Bender, you might have one."

"That's my point. Wait till we know. You simmer down and I'll give you the word if anything breaks. I ought to clap you in a cell."

"I'll stay out of sight. No cell necessary."

"Where'll you be?"

I thought a minute, then gave him the Fairview number. We jawed a few more minutes, and I left.

Morning found me at Fairview, a lowercase shell of Shell Scott. What with framblotting and everything, I had got very little sleep. And I'd spent over two hours at City Hall before coming back to join Laurel, who was still asleep beside me. Right now detectives in Reno, Las Vegas, and all over Nevada were looking for Brad Bender. Or his body. More were hunting for the so-called Bob Brown. There was quite a bit of activity — but as Sam had made clear, there was now little for me to do until I heard from him. Or Nevada. As long as I was supposed to sit around and wait, this seemed as good a place as any other. Laurel sighed softly in her sleep. A better place, I thought.

She opened her eyes and blinked at me. "Hi."

"Hi."

"What time is it?"

I turned, looked at the clock on the small table. "Almost five."

"Oh, we'd better get up. Big day. Calisthenics, breakfast. This is July 3, you know. Convention starts today."

"So it does," I mumbled.

"You going to be here? I can tell you everything the health director was — *is* — supposed to do."

"I'll be here a while. But is it so damned important that you have a health director?"

"Oh, no tragedy if we don't. But it would be so much nicer, Shell. Really it would. I talked to Mr. and Mrs. Blore last night and they want you here." She grinned. "They said you'd be better than nothing. And you might enjoy it. You'd have to judge the games and races — and the beauty contest."

"Beauty contest? That's right. Well, I might be around awhile. A little while. Until, and unless, I get a phone call I'm expecting. Can't do much this early anyway, can I?"

"Uh-uh." She was smiling. A moment later she said, "No, no. We've got to get up."

Well, I got through the calisthenics without much trouble. I had about two hundred in the class, since a number of conventioneers had arrived the night before and bunked in the green dressing room, where all the convention guests would leave their clothing. Extra cots had been placed in the two other buildings and in the cabins for them. The calisthenics were short and sweet today. And I didn't mind so much this time. I was turning into a real dyed-out-of-the-wool nudist.

By nine A.M. the sun was warm and it had turned into a beautiful balmy day, with a startlingly blue sky tufted with puffy white clouds. Earlier I'd spent half an hour with the Council, being briefed on upcoming events and my place in them. I'd called the Headquarters a couple of times and talked to Samson, but the status quo remained.

One odd thing came out in the Council meeting. Between three and four hundred sunbathers from all over the United States were expected. Over the past months Mr. and Mrs. Blore had taken pains to see that printed cards of invitation were mailed to all who had expressed their intention to be here for the big day. Each card entitled two people — one couple — to admittance and would pass them through the gate; much care had been taken to see that only approved naturists, most of them members of the American Sunbathing Association, received cards. Everything seemed set for an orderly gathering, except for one thing: Four admittance cards couldn't be accounted for. That info came out at the Council meeting, but I let it drift from my mind in the hectic hours that followed immediately.

By nine o'clock almost everybody scheduled to arrive had put in an appearance. Laurel and I had stayed together all morning, and now we were at the center of the clearing in the middle of much jovial conversation and loud helloes as old friends and acquaintances greeted and slapped each other on the back. High on the back.

Laurel and I stood near a long table that groaned under the weight of fresh fruits and vegetables, cold meats, nuts, and bottles of goop. In its center was an enormous punch bowl of freshly squeezed fruit juices. Several yards away was a wooden platform that I understood had something to do with one of the contests. And all around us were naked people. Half of them must have been men, but all I could see were women.

To be perfectly honest, the overall quality of the 150 or so females present wasn't as high as I had become accustomed to in these last two days in Fairview. One gal a few feet away had nothing on top but damn near everything on the bottom; it looked like the butt that jokes were made of.

The scene, needless to say, had never bounced against my eyeballs before, and it made me think a bit. I've spent all my life in Hollywood and I'd about decided that one of the things wrong with the place and its women is deception — which might well have been one of the reasons I was beginning to appreciate Fairview. I've been out with some Hollywood babes whose battle cry should have been "Sham on you," babes who looked incredible and were. It's like peeling an artichoke to get down to where you're going — girdles, stays, foam rubber. Sometimes there's so much stuff you begin to think there'll be nothing down there but a midget laughing.

Not here, though. Here was one place you couldn't take it with you unless you had it to begin with. I took Laurel by her soft brown arm and pulled her with me toward the punch bowl.

"Come on, honey. My throat's dry. Let's have some beet juice."

We weaved through the press of people to the big punch bowl and scooped out two cups of the reddish fluid.

Laurel sipped at her drink and said, "Good turnout, isn't it?"

"Dandy. More arriving all the time." I swallowed at my punch and frowned. It wasn't beet juice. It was delicious and cold, and it had a slightly familiar taste. "What's in this?" I said. "Most likely I imagined it, but I thought I tasted something stronger than carrots. About a hundred proof."

"You mean whisky?" Her brows pulled way down over the bright blue eyes.

"Something like that. Whisky, gin, vodka. Hard to tell in all this muck."

"Oh, Shell. Nobody'd spike the punch. Not here."

I guessed she was right. So I tossed my juices off, and then Laurel and I both had another cup and wandered around looking at the scenery.

Near the green dressing room was a long table loaded with all kinds of fireworks, everything from ladyfingers through skyrockets and Roman candles to aerial bombs. A box of extra-long waxed matches, together with sticks of punk, was on the table's edge. I knew that they were for tonight's wind-up of the first day's convention festivities, and rather hoped I'd be here to see the show. I'm crazy about fireworks. I was looking at them when I thought I heard something odd.

"What's that?" I said. "Was that something tootling?"

"You mean the music? The Sacramento group's band must have started playing. Hard to hear in all this conversation."

There was a constant muffled roar of voices beating against my eardrums all the time, but I listened. "There it is," I said. "Another tootle."

"I heard it. Good, the band's going to start."

Suddenly what she'd said got through to me. My eyes snapped open wide and I found myself grinning. "Band? Music? You mean dancing!"

"No, silly. There isn't going to be any dancing. It's a band, not an orchestra. You know, tuba and piccolo and bass drum and so on. It's for the community sing later, and just for fun. Besides, in all this noise there has to be something loud to signal the start of each event."

Even though I was disappointed that there wasn't going to be dancing, I had to admit that the *oompah-oompah* added that extra something to the general hilarity. Then, for the merest fraction of a second, everything went slightly out of focus. Pain flickered inside my still tender skull.

I shook my head. "Honey doll," I said, "this beet juice has fermented. I think."

She gave me an odd look. We'd both finished our second cups of punch, and as if by common consent we walked back to the bowl. There wasn't a great deal left, but we got some more, and now the fermented taste was really strong. I swallowed and grinned widely at Laurel. "What do you know? Some fiend did spike the punch after all."

There was a great blast from the band.

Laurel said, "There it is. Hurry. You've got to be there."

"Where, where?"

"There. The race." She turned and trotted away from me, weaving through the crowd.

"What race?" I yelled, and started weaving after her. I really was weaving. Then I remembered. She'd told me about it. This was a foot race to choose Miss Speedy of the Fairview Convention.

We burst out from the edge of the crowd and I noticed a great mass of women gathering in a straight line about fifty yards to my left. More women were running toward them, getting into position. Laurel ran to the right.

I caught up with her when she stopped, but she said, "This is the finish line, Shell. You stand right here. I'll be there" — she pointed — "and Mr. Blore, the third judge, will be there." She pointed in the opposite direction. "You'll be in the middle."

"I'll . . . be in the middle?"

"Yes. We'll all three be right here on the finish line."

I noticed a string laid out on the ground at our feet. Laurel pointed again, at right angles to the line and toward what was now a seething mass of women. There were at least fifty of them. I could hear them squealing and shouting even though they were at least a hundred yards away. On our left the nonparticipants were forming another mass to watch.

Laurel went on, "You'll be in the middle, where you'll have the best chance to see which girl wins, but Mr. Blore and I will be at opposite ends of the finish line in case a girl close to us crosses the line first." She paused and blinked. "I feel woozy."

There was another blast from the band. It terrified me. I gasped. "You mean I'll be in the middle — and they're going to run at me? What if they run me down?"

"They won't."

"I don't know about that. They might run me down and trample on me. I can think of better ways to get massacred."

A bugle blew, cracking on the high note.

Laurel said, "That's the warning. Next one is the start. Get ready." She ran away.

I looked dazedly around. Mr. Blore was already in place, and Laurel had reached the far end of the finish line. A bugle sounded again, loud and clear.

There was a monstrous, blood-chilling shriek from my left and I snapped my head around. I stared. A mountain of flesh was in motion, coming at me. At first it was a pink landslide, a volcanic lava flow of flesh rolling this way to inundate me; then I began to pick out individual segments of the mass: women. Women, all running as if each absolutely had to win, arms flying, legs pumping, everything doing something.

It was appalling. Never in my wildest moments had I ever dreamed of anything remotely like this. There was a sound of thunder like buffalo stampeding; a trumpeting as of elephants stuck in swamps.

Suddenly the race was over. I didn't have any idea who had won.

All I knew was that three figures had streaked past me — and then I was drowning in naked babes. Bedlam and Babel were right here, all around me. *Swish* and a form flew past; *whoosh* and another body veered around me. Squeals and more squeals and laughter and shouts billowed in the air.

I just lay there, my mouth hanging open like a trap door, while with something approaching horror I thought: I am losing my interest in women!

Suddenly three girls were standing over me. They were all arguing pleasantly and looking down at me — yeah, down; I was flat on my back staring at the sky — and all three said in unison, "I won, didn't I? Didn't I?"

I got to my feet and looked down at them for a change. I made a snap decision.

"You won," I said, pointing to the girl in the middle. "You won by — er — a nose."

She clapped her hands. The prize was a pair of silver wings for her feet, but she should have been awarded a platinum brassiere. She had practically no nose at all.

They left, the losers accepting my decision with good grace. And then Laurel was beside me. She said, "Well, that was fun."

I laughed hollowly. All my life I had thought that something like this would be the ultimate, the crest, the absolute unsurpassable peak. Now it had happened, and it had been horrible.

Laurel said, "I'm glad you spotted the winner. Neither Mr. Blore nor I could see into the middle."

"Baby." My voice was thin. "I'll tell you the truth. After the first wave, the shock troops, everything went blank. I was knocked down and trampled on. They streamed by forever. You have no idea . . . " I stopped, then came to a decision. "Laurel, I'm going to have some more of those vegetable drippings. And I hope it *is* spiked. I hope it's poisoned."

Laurel followed me to the punch bowl. I was scraping a cup against the bottom of the thing when she arrived. "Gone!" I cried. "All gone!" My brain felt loose inside my skull. "Laurel," I said, "I resign. I'm done. I'm a shambles. This is the — "

A crash of sound came from the band.

"*No!*" I shouted. "I won't!"

"Shell," Laurel said sharply. "Don't talk like that. Come on." She took me by the hand. "Hurry."

She started pulling me after her, talking as we shoved through the milling crowd. "This is the beauty contest. It's really the most important contest of the whole day. You can't miss it."

"Beauty contest. I was looking forward to it once. But the joy has gone out of — "

"Hurry," she said. In moments we were there.

We were at the little platform I'd noticed earlier in the morning. It was about fifteen feet long and six feet wide, up about a yard off the ground, made of pine planks nailed together. There were no sides to it, so you could look right underneath it easily, though there seemed little point in doing it, and at each end were three wooden steps.

Laurel said, "We've got a few minutes yet. I wanted to explain the procedure. See those steps? There are twenty-two girls, one from each camp represented here. One at a time they'll walk up the steps on one side, onto the platform, then across it."

"They come across up there on the platform?" I was silent for a moment. "Maybe I'll judge this affair after all."

"They come across slowly to here" — Laurel pointed to the steps on our left — "and then go down the steps. We three — you, Mr. Blore, and I as last year's queen — judge them, compare our ratings, and announce the winner. I'll be right here beside you if you need any explanation. It's really very simple. Oh, here they come."

They were on their way. A few minutes later all was fairly quiet. Mr. Blore, Laurel, and I sat in wooden chairs before the stand. The twenty-two girls lined up, one behind the other, at the right-hand steps. The whole bunch of conventioneers was scattered in back of us on the grass. The band was on the far side of the stand, playing, not just blasting away now, but playing real music. At least they were carrying a tune. After much concentration I recognized "Stardust."

Nice. Gave everything a touch of real class. The band stopped, a bugle sounded, then the band reverted to "Stardust" again. I had calmed down quite a bit by now, but everything was a little woozy. Oh, I could see well enough. As a matter of fact, I had already picked out a little redhead who looked like a winner. And I was beginning to wonder what was going on in the outside world.

A man — an old, old man — was waiting by the phone in the event that a call came for me. But none had. Last night and again during my few unhectic moments this morning I had thought about the fact that to the killer of Mrs. Redstone and of Yates, the would-be killer of Laurel and of me, I was the one guy who still had to be knocked off. But since I was staying out of action, so to speak, I figured that this was the one place where hoods couldn't get at me, the one place where I'd be safe. No hoods, I figured, would come in *here* for me. Which just goes to show the lengths guys will go to when it's really important to kill a man. They arrived at ten o'clock, straight up.

As the first girl walked up the steps and started mincing slowly across the platform, I settled back to judge a real, down-to-earth, honest-to-goodness beauty contest. Nobody was going to tap-dance in this one. The first gal wasn't bad; she paused in the middle of the platform and turned slowly around, then went on down the steps on our left. The second girl started up. The band finished "Stardust" and swung into its opening bars again. I had a hunch I was going to get tired of "Stardust."

I glanced at the band and noticed a guy standing near the musicians with his back to me. There was something vaguely familiar about him, but my mind was on other things, and I turned my attention back to those other things. The redhead, who, as far as I was concerned, had won, stood next in line. I don't know how I happened to notice; I just looked to my right. Two groups of people had shifted their positions so that temporarily there was an open space between them, and beyond them I saw a couple that seemed somehow different from the rest. A man and a woman were standing apart from the others, both carrying small leather bags, like briefcases. As I watched, each of them reached into a case and pulled out a piece of brown cloth. I thought: What the hell? And then I really saw something funny.

They slipped the cloths over their heads and suddenly they were wearing brown hoods with eyeholes they could look through. That was strange. A rather amusing thought struck me then. Even if they'd been friends of mine, and even if the girl had been a *very* good friend of mine, I wouldn't have been able to recognize them, or later say who they'd been. There is a kind of anonymity among nudists, and nudists with hoods on their heads are about as anonymous as you can get. It's the fault of our stuffy society, of course, but that's the way it is, and I'd never realized before how true it was. I was philosophical as the devil.

And, too, I was full of fruit juice. Which maybe is what made me think I saw the gun. The man dropped his briefcase and something tumbled out of it, a something he quickly grabbed and shoved back into the case. That gave me another chuckle. Suppose a criminal nudist, one among four or five hundred nudists, put a hood over his face and shot somebody. Off with the hood's hood, he leaves — and he's safe. Who could ever identify him? How in hell could anybody here at Fairview, say, later identify the character in court? I got a big kick out of it.

Chuckling, I looked back at my redhead — and then came the first cracked note, the first inkling of real screaming pandemonium.

"Stardust" had ended. The band was playing something different for a change. And over there near the line of girls I saw a woman's face that jarred me, though at first I didn't know why. There was something vaguely familiar about it, and also about the tune the band was playing.

What with the *oompahs* and all the rest it took me a few seconds to figure out what the melody was. And by that time it was too late to stop it, to stop anything, for that matter.

Suddenly I recognized that slow, draggy *Oompah, poo-pah-pah* and sprang to my feet. Now I knew who that big guy at the band had been. I'd seen sunlight glinting off his completely bald head — the bald head of Young Egg Foo.

And the band was playing "St. Louis Blues."

"No! Stop the music!" I yelled.

But I was too late. The band kept playing. And there, suddenly, was Babe Le Toot.

22

I just stood there, paralyzed, staring at Babe up there on the platform in place of my redhead; Babe in all her glory — and drunk as a lord.

I knew, all at once, what Foo had been doing near the band, what those brown hoods were for, what had happened to those swiped admission cards. Maybe even what had happened to some of that punch. Babe was so drunk she thought the platform was U-shaped.

She was weaving around now, grinning and winking, snorting and chuckling. Any minute she was going to do some bumps and grinds. She was in her element at last, and it was a heating element. She started doing some little ones, gently, as if she were merely waving at the audience, but then she went back to the rear of the platform, raised one hand over her head and drew back her entire midsection.

It was one of those moments.

I couldn't have yanked my eyes away for anything. One of the greatest bumps ever seen was about to be bumped.

I knew, I just knew, that this was going to be an epic bump, one to cherish in memory. She was wound up to put her all into this one, years of training and "St. Louis Blues" conditioning.

But Babe was out of practice. The weight hanging in back there overbalanced her and slowly she toppled backward. She lit on her head and just lay there.

That broke the spell. I sprang to the platform, but staggered woozily, and that fool band began playing "Stardust" again.

I swung around, yelling for silence, for attention — which you can bet I was getting — and the band stopped. It was suddenly quiet and I had my chance:

"It's Foo!" I shouted. "And Babe Le Toot, too!"

The echo of my voice came back from the hills like the whistle of a faraway locomotive. People ogled me, but didn't move. The fools didn't believe me. I shouted, "It is *too*, Foo. And Toot. Ah, the hell with it. They're criminals! Who cares what their names are? They're hoods! All those guys with hoods on are hoods!"

Several people drew back from the front of the platform, then a shot rang out and everybody drew back, me included, because the slug whistled past my ear, and suddenly I was six feet off the ground, clutching handfuls of air. I never needed a gun more badly.

I ran through milling people, headed toward my cabin, where my clothes and gun were. I didn't make it. As I neared the green dressing room another hooded guy stepped through the door and aimed a gun at me. He not only aimed it, he fired it. I hit the grass hard, rolling and feeling pain slide over my arm and shoulder and inside my head; then I crashed into a table and fireworks fell all over.

As I got to my feet the guy left the doorway and started toward me, not running, just walking closer and closer. There was no need for him to hurry; he could take his time about shooting me. I turned to run in the opposite direction and saw another guy loping toward me, a gun in his right fist too. He had a brown cloth over his head, but I knew it was big Foo. Beyond him the scene was indescribable, people running left and right and around in circles, shrieking and falling down.

It was a hell of a last sight on earth, but I was damned if I'd just stand here and let those guys fire at me. Fire . . . And fireworks all around me. Maybe, by God, this was already the Fourth of July. The matches were still on the table. I grabbed one, struck it, and latched onto a handful of Roman candles, lighting them all at once and grabbing more in my other hand as the fuses started sputtering.

There was a noise like *thoo* and a big ball of burning powder shot out of one of the candles almost in my face. Foo was only about fifteen yards away; the other guy was even closer and walking slowly forward. The fools didn't know I was armed. As the ball of fire sizzled into the air, the guy coming from the dressing room looked up at it. By the time he looked down again I had about a dozen of my weapons aimed at him, all of them lighted by now.

Balls of fire started whooshing out at him like shells from a small rocket launcher. Only one of the balls hit him, but he let out a yelp and fell over backward. I turned and ran straight at Foo, practically enveloped in smoke and flame. I'll swear that all of those Roman candles let loose at once and blazing pellets bounced off Foo like incandescent peanuts. I kept running as he whirled and brought his hands up before his face — but he didn't let go of his gun.

I swerved and ran to the left of him and past. Someone shot at me again and missed. I ran like a deer, still hanging onto the Roman candles, which were sputtering and fizzling. I was almost out of ammunition. A sudden staccato burst of noise rattled behind me and I thought one of the slobs had got his hands on a machine gun and was mowing me down. But nothing hit me. I glanced over my shoulder to see skyrockets zipping all over the place. Roman candles sending fireballs bouncing along the ground and flames going up from the stand where the fireworks had been stacked. I also saw *three* guys running after me now. Guns glinted in the hands of all three.

In among the trees I kept going fast enough, but my lungs felt stretched like used gum and my head throbbed. A gunshot cracked and bark flew from a tree on my right. I saw water ahead of me. The pool. I had run into the damned blind canyon. And I sure as hell couldn't go up that cliff. I couldn't get back out of here now, either. When I turned I saw a man coming through the passageway.

I was trapped.

But then I saw my ladder in the sky. No, I wasn't trapped. Not me. Not old Eekle from Arcturus.

23

Everything in those next few seconds was, and will always remain, blurred in my mind. I remember running toward the rope that anchored those balloons, spotting the hunting knife I'd left on the ground the night before, grabbing it, and looping one leg over a rung of the rope ladder. A slug pinked my arm at almost the instant I slashed the rope holding down the balloons. And then zoop, I was airborne.

I didn't go up with really tremendous speed, though at first it seemed to me that I was hurtling through space like a meteor because I was upside down and dangling by one leg. But when I managed to grab the ropes and haul myself upright I was still only about fifty feet off the ground. I looked down. All three of the men had yanked off their hoods, probably to see better, and one of them, neck craned up — even from where I was I could see the gaping hole that was his mouth — was still running. He ran right into the water. The two other guys were stock-still, arms hanging at their sides and heads bent back almost far enough to snap.

I hoped I'd get out of pistol range before they recovered their senses, but suddenly Foo yanked up his gun and started popping away at me. I was really in a hell of a position. Only two shots were fired, though; Foo must have used up his other bullets during the chase.

At the last shot there was a little puffing noise above me and I looked up. A couple of my balloons sighed softly and collapsed. I sort of collapsed a little too. But my craft kept carrying me skyward. A mild wondering thought about when and where this would stop occurred to me, but then I looked down at the earth again. Three little men looked up at me; one shook his fist. I raised my eyes and looked over the trees to the clearing, and what I saw drove all other thoughts from my mind.

Never had I seen or read or heard or thought of such a wild vista. Over four hundred naked people, their bodies white against the green grass, were streaking every which way. I was still close enough to pick out details, and I saw that many were on the ground, rolling aimlessly, and lots more were beating their heads with their hands while still others were hanging onto friends.

Faintly I could hear a string of poppety-pops. The fireworks stand was blazing and as I watched a streak of smoke soared into the sky and blossomed into arching, many-colored fireballs. But there was a great deal more smoke than even the fireworks could account for.

Beyond the stand the roof of the dressing room was blazing. I was sort of numb, but I knew that inside it were all the clothes of all the visiting conventioneers.

But that was getting farther and farther from me. I was way up in the air and a stiff wind was blowing, pushing me along. I didn't seem to be going any higher, just moving over the scenery below at a fast clip. It was fairly easy to hang onto the rope ladder, both feet securely placed on separate rungs, but it wasn't exactly comfortable.

Time passed. I thought some more about the case, and several things got clearer. I dwelt on the fact that Samson had said that Brad Bender was, among other things, a cackle-bladder expert. A "cackle bladder" is a little bag of chicken blood that a con man puts into his mouth and bites on when somebody fires a pistol filled with blank cartridges at him. Blood squirts out of his mouth and the guy who fired the blank thinks he's killed him.

I also put a couple of dates together: Yates's report to "Client" was dated June 14; and on June 15, "Bob Brown" and his "wife" had entered Fairview. I was quite pleased with my mental processes. It helps to get off by yourself. Now I knew all the answers; this was a dandy time for it. I noted casually that, as usual, the wind was blowing from Fairview toward L.A.

And then I grabbed my ladder and clung to it, crying out hoarsely. Los Angeles? *Los Angeles?* I got cold all over. All over. Not that. But, yes, there was Figueroa Boulevard. There was Sunset. I could pick out the City Hall, towering high over everything else. As minutes passed I could even make out people down there in the streets. It must have been a big bargain day in the stores, there were so many people. As I watched, the mass of people got even bigger. Yeah, it was some bargain day, all right.

My mind was like mush. The strain was beginning to tell on me. The events of these last days, calisthenics and killers and races, that goddamned fruit juice — everything had conspired to turn my brain into oatmeal. Suddenly my eyes bugged and it actually seemed as though something snapped in my head. I knew, then, what had happened: This was a dream. It wasn't true. I was making it all up. This couldn't be happening. I wasn't up in the air, a soaring nudist, floating toward the Civic Center. Ah, but I was.

The sidewalks were crowded; people below were even thronging in the middle of the streets. Somehow I was much lower now, sinking, and the sinking sensation I had now made the last one seem like a rising sensation. I could see the people very clearly, but that wasn't the worst of it. Traffic had stopped. Way up here on my perch I could hear horns blowing. The distant sound of a crash reached my ears. No, not all the traffic had stopped. Directly below me there was a police car, keeping pace with my progress. Its siren was wailing continually. I, too, was wailing continually.

I had dropped much lower, even lower than the top of City Hall, which was pretty close at this point. Awfully close. It seemed appropriate that I was on about the same level with its twenty-fifth floor. The observation tower is on the twenty-fifth floor.

And then my mind tottered. I told myself over and over that this was impossible. That nothing could make it happen. Not even freak winds could make it truly happen.

But I had to accept it. The winds were right, the height was perfect. Years from now, when this tale was told, few of the coming generation would believe it. But it was true. I was going to float through space like a Zeppelin and moor at City Hall.

I had the feeling that Civil Defense was watching me, marking my progress on a chart. In panic I tried to figure a way out. Maybe I could make people think I was a visitor from another planet. A less thickly inhibited planet. Maybe I could float in through a window and babble gibberish as I had done with Laurel and they'd all bow down. I imagined the *Examiner* putting out an extra: "Saucer Man Arrives in Strange Craft!"

Then I thought: My God, what if Civil Defense reports me and the Air Force shoots me down? At that very instant a jet plane swooped past me and on toward the horizon. I almost lost my grip on the ladder. Those balloons above me probably looked like a squadron of flying discs — and they'd captured a human!

I heard noises, shouts. Slowly I came back from wherever I'd been. Smack in front of me was the wall of City Hall, dotted with people yelping from windows. One ass was leaning out and laughing so hard I thought he was going to fall fifteen stories. I looked down. Nothing but people.

You couldn't even see the goddamned grass around City Hall. Just a mass of upturned faces. And open mouths. And pointing fingers.

Ten feet away from me now, in an open window, was a man with a cigarette dangling from his lips and lighter in his hand. Suddenly I thought of all that gas up there above me.

"Don't!" I shouted. "Don't light it! I'm a bomb, a human bomb. I'll blow up City Hall, blow it down!"

If that happened, people would be sure I was a Russian secret weapon. Or a weapon from the Moon. Even a Martian. If I blew up, space travel would be set back a hundred years. People would cry: "The Martians are bombs!"

A lot of secretaries had their heads stuck out of windows. Most of them were screaming, but the little hypocrites were still looking. I recognized some of them, but by now I hardly cared. One big-eyed blonde, even bigger-eyed now than usual, recognized me in turn.

She pointed. "It is!" she screeched. "No, it isn't. My God, it is! It's Shell Scott!"

24

I nearly died of embarrassment. She didn't have to make it so obvious. But then I was banged into the building's side, and hands reached for me and pulled me into an office. Three secretaries ran out the door. Pushing through the crowd came some uniformed officers, some in plain clothes. I saw Captain Samson, his usually pink face a brighter hue. Alongside him was Lieutenant Rawlins, a good friend of mine. Once he had been a good friend of mine. He was laughing like hell.

I stuck my face close to his. "Well, what's so funny?"

That did it. The bastard choked and gurgled and finally sank to the floor on his fanny, roaring like an idiot, hands wrapped around his sides.

Sam stopped squarely in front of me, a cigar in his mouth. Slowly his teeth ground together. The cigar bent, then fell to the floor. "Shell," he said in a voice taut with emotion. "Shell, you've done some crazy things before, but really, this is too much."

"I've got to get back to the nudist camp," I burbled. Well, what would you have said? Sam kept biting his cigar stub. More hilarious cops were in the room now. Guys slapped their thighs. Somehow we got out of there and I wound up in a police uniform that Rawlins found somewhere for me.

Then we were down in Room 42 and Sam was saying, "Well, let's go over to the jail."

"Sam, I've been trying to tell you. We've got the whole thing. I've got to get out of here and — "

"We *have* to throw you in jail. All those people . . . " He shrugged helplessly.

Five minutes later I was still arguing, still explaining. Sam had told me that they'd picked up Brad Bender in Las Vegas and he'd been brought to City Hall half an hour before. The crime lab had reported that the stain in the nap of Norman's carpet was blood, all right; but not human blood.

"I tried to call you," Samson said. "Couldn't even get an answer at that number. Something happened to the phone. I didn't know you were . . . I didn't know you were . . . " He threw his hands in the air.

"Sam, listen. Throw me in jail later if you've got to, but right now let me talk to Bender. We know the slug tossed at me was from the gun that killed Yates. We know Mrs. Redstone didn't kill herself. We know almost all of it. Let me have two minutes with Bender, and we'll pick up the killer. Then I'll go to a monastery. Join the Foreign Legion."

I won. Bender was brought into Room 42. I handed Rawlins the gun in my uniform holster, winked at Sam, and said, "I've got five minutes in your office alone with this bastard before you come in, right?"

"Right."

"Pay no attention to any odd noises."

"Naturally not," he said.

Bender looked pale. He was about six feet tall, broad-shouldered and handsome, as are a lot of con men. He had plenty of wavy black hair, graying at the temples. His hands were manacled in front of him, the cuffs slipped under his belt so that he couldn't raise his arms.

He shifted his feet nervously. "What's coming off?"

"Can't you guess, Bender?"

He swallowed. "Look, I don't get this. I haven't done anything. All of a damn sudden you haul me back to L.A." He paused. "You can't get away with working me over in there." He jerked his head toward the inner office, and his voice was firm and confident. His face wasn't so confident, though.

He was right, of course. I couldn't work him over. Sam wouldn't have allowed it in the first place. But the important thing was to make him think I could get away with it. I said, "Maybe not, Bender. But I can give it a good try. Unless you want to spill the story of your phony murder. We know you're a cackle-bladder expert. And we know Andon Poupelle's supposed to have knocked you off. He still thinks you're dead, doesn't he?" I paused. "Take your pick, Bender. We know it all anyway."

He looked at me, then at Samson.

"The way I see it, Bender, it was just a gag. Wasn't that it?" I looked at Sam. "He won't do time, will he? If that's all the deal turns out to be?"

Sam said to me, not looking at Bender, "I can't promise anything. It would look good, though, if he cooperated with the police. He knows that."

Bender said, "You talk to Poupelle?"

I hesitated, then said, "I'll give it to you straight. We can't even find the guy. Maybe he's dead for all I know."

He chewed his lip, seemed to make up his mind. "He's in Vegas. Some friends told me, but he didn't see me there."

"Was Ed Norman the friend who told you?"

"Naturally." He squinted at me. "It was a gag, remember. Here's how it went: Norman said we'd play a joke on Poupelle. Night of June 2 we all three were in Norman's office at the castle. Norman made sure there was a gun on his desk, loaded with blanks. I slipped the cackle bladder in my mouth. We rigged a fight, made it look good. I was choking Norman. He managed to yell at Poupelle to grab the gun. Poupelle plugged me and I staggered toward him, squirted blood all over him. You know the rest."

"Yeah." In Bender's language all the niceties and high points of the confidence man's technique were left out. Andon would have been played like a fish, ready for the psychological moment. He'd have grabbed the gun, fired at Bender — fired a blank — and Bender then would have bit on the cackle bladder. I could see the rest: blood spurting through his lips over Poupelle, over Bender's chin, blood all over, messy as hell. He'd have groaned a little, kicked a couple of times, and expired artistically. Bender had died that way about fifty times in his career, and nobody had ever thought he wasn't as dead as King Tut.

While Bender talked, Sam was on the phone, making sure that a couple of police cars would be in readiness down front. Bender said, "That's about all. What happened after that I wouldn't know. Norman sent me to Vegas, told me to stay there till he got in touch. It was a gag, remember."

"Sure," I said. "Only Poupelle didn't know it, and Norman held that fake murder over his head, made him do exactly what he wanted him to do."

Rawlins handed me back my gun and I slid it into the holster, pulled the uniform coat I was wearing down tighter onto my shoulders.

Samson hung up and said to me, "The boys picked Bender up in a car, you know, on his way out of Vegas. He almost made it."

I swung toward Bender and said, "I thought you told me you were to stay there until Norman gave you the word. He call you?"

"No." Bender swallowed. "I heard the noise that cops were on my tail. Before I took off, I called Norman here, told him I was blowing, and why."

"Let's go," Sam said.

"Just a second." I looked at Bender. "What time did you call, friend?"

"Just before they picked me up. Maybe nine-thirty this morning."

We left Bender with one of the officers and ran out the door. Two police cars were parked at the Main Street entrance. Samson slid behind the wheel of one and I sat up front with him, other officers piling into the second car. Sam jerked the wheel and gunned out from the curb in a U-turn, hit the siren, and swung left into Sunset, headed for Figueroa.

"At first I thought Poupelle blasted Yates to keep him from messing up Andon's play for the Redstone dough," I said. "Figured Norman learned about it and was bleeding the guy. Like that loan from Offenbrand. Poupelle got a hundred and fifty Gs — but Norman deposited it. Finally there was so much pointing at Norman a blind man could see it."

Sam braked, let up on the pedal, and skidded into Figueroa. I opened my eyes, relaxed my legs, and said "When I learned about Poupelle's dropping fifty Gs at the castle, I went out to see Norman about it. Yates also learned that item of info from Three Eyes — so Three Eyes told me — and Yates obviously would have done the same thing I did: call on Norman. Norman got to Yates, maybe with money, or the promise of big money, and Yates sold out, started working for Norman. If Norman had managed to kill me he might have got away with his caper. He made his big try at me today, but it missed, too, because . . . We won't go into that."

Sam swung onto Forrest Street, leading toward the castle. He said, "Think he's got any idea we're on our way?"

"Well, Bender phoned him from Vegas, so he'll be jerky as hell. Not for fear Poupelle might see or talk to him — Andon's in so deep now it wouldn't make any difference — but because Norman will know the whole story's about to pop. Especially with me still alive. Right after Bender's call he sent four of his boys out to polish me off, remember." I stopped.

In a second I went on, "Hell, yes, he knows, Sam. Even if his boys didn't get back to the castle he knows by now that I've talked to Bender, talked again to the police."

"How you figure . . . Oh. Yeah."

Yeah, indeed. By this time probably half the United States knew that Shell Scott had visited City Hall from heaven.

The car went over the hill and started down. We could see the castle from here. Sam said, "There's a chance he's already flown. But once he runs he's got to keep on running, and he knows it. So he'll take as much of his stuff, including money, with him as he can."

I said, "There's the little matter of a guy called Offie, too, and — "

We both saw it at the same time, a car racing out over the drawbridge, careening right, heading toward us. Sam had cut the siren once we were out of traffic and now he said, "Must be him." I looked at his face and saw his shaggy brows pull down, that cast-iron chin jut out farther. He didn't slow down.

"Eight to five," I said. "But I can't figure why he's coming this way."

"Highway Patrol's alerted, roadblocks; that way we'd have him in minutes. Must be figuring he might make it into town, drop out of sight there."

Norman, if it was Norman, would have seen us by now, and the other car behind us. He was damned close. I swallowed. "Sam. Can't we stop, swing sideways? Block the road?"

He kept his foot clear down on the accelerator. "He'll stop."

"Yeah, all over us."

"We stop, and he just turns around, hightails it off. Maybe some good cop gets hurt."

"Sam, you're a good cop." My voice was wiggling. "And I'm not such a bad guy, even after . . ."

I couldn't finish it. That long black car looked like a locomotive on our track. We were in the middle of the road, no more than forty or fifty yards separating the two cars, when Sam hit the siren and it burst into sound like a thousand banshees. I saw Norman's car veer, heard his tires screech. He swung clear off the road and went by us on our left. Only inches away I could see his face bent over the steering wheel.

I thought he was going to make it, but the car skidded, kicked up dirt at the right of the road. Then the brakes of our car were squealing and I was thrown against the door as Sam did something incredible, at least something that I'd never have tried.

Then we were skidding sideways, our collective rear end swinging around so that for a full second we were pointing back the way we'd come but the car went on sliding. Sam didn't even kill the engine, only jerked gears and jazzed the motor, and then we were heading after Norman, gaining speed in a hurry.

I didn't try to say anything; there was no talking to Samson when he was driving like this. But now I saw Norman's car far off the road, right wheels in a ditch. The car door stood open. I spotted him, running up the weed-covered hillside toward a clump of trees and thick brush, a gun in his hand. Sam slammed on the brakes and I was out the door and running before the car stopped.

Norman got into the trees long before I did, but I pounded ahead at full speed. I meant to kill that boy if I got half a chance. At this moment I blamed him for all my troubles, which at least was enough to keep me running. Then I was in the shadows of the trees. I stopped.

There wasn't any sound. I cocked the police revolver, wishing I had my own .38. Then slowly I walked forward, trying to look everywhere at once.

The next time I stopped I heard something rustle on my left and spun in that direction, crouching, the gun held before me, my elbow pressed against my side.

There wasn't anything there. Just a fist-sized rock still rolling over the ground. For a split second it didn't register; I didn't realize I'd been caught by one of the oldest tricks in the world, a tossed pebble to make a man look the wrong way. But it was for only a split second. I was still turning when I saw the pebble, and I stopped, but the next instant I dived forward flat on the ground, the dirt slapping my face and scraping my skin. It sounded as if the gun blasted almost in my ear; dirt geysered inches to the right of my head.

I rolled that way, hoping he'd have jerked the gun toward me and that he'd have expected me to move in the opposite direction. Because he had me cold if I didn't cross him up that little bit. As I rolled I squirmed onto my back, and before I even caught sight of him I squeezed the trigger on the police revolver twice, not aiming at anything but praying that just the sudden violent sound might jar him.

Maybe that was what did it. His gun cracked again and he missed me, though I felt the hot wind hiss past my cheek. Then I saw him, and I was firing again even before my gun was pointed at him. But it was pointed at Norman's body before the gun clicked empty. I hit him twice.

He jackknifed forward but didn't go down. The gun dropped from his fingers and he slapped both hands against his middle and staggered backward one step. Then he tried to straighten up, blood oozing thickly through his fingers. He couldn't make it.

He stood facing me, bent over, his head raised so he could see me. His mouth moved and a stream of obscenity poured out. Then his knees buckled and he crumpled, still holding his hands over his belly. My throat was dry and rougher than sandpaper as I walked to him and squatted before him. Samson had plowed up just as Norman fell; right behind him were four other officers.

I doubt that Norman even knew they were there. He was half on his side, one elbow partly supporting him. I said, "You've had it, Norman. Go out clammed, or tell it. It's too late for anything else now."

He told me what to do. Then he coughed. Coughed blood, and he knew there was a hole in his lung. "It doesn't hurt," he said slowly, a note of surprise in his voice. "I'll make it. I'll — "

"You're dead, Norman. You're in shock, that's all. I give you a minute, maybe two."

His face was pale, a film of perspiration making it shiny. He tried to shake his head. "You're lying. I'll . . . " Then a soft sigh came from his throat and his eyes widened a little. He got a blank, staring look and I saw his Adam's apple move convulsively.

I'd seen that look a dozen times. There's nothing else like it — the expression on a man's face when he knows he's on the way out. Norman knew; somewhere in his brain something cold had burst and spread. He knew he was dying.

Then he started talking. I'd seen that before, too, the words coming all in a rush, piling up on each other, some of them just sounds, not words at all. Maybe when there's so little time, they suddenly have to say more than anyone really says in a lifetime. They never make it; Norman didn't.

A lot of what he did get out was disjointed, but it was more than enough. He said that Poupelle had come out to the castle near the end of May with Vera Redstone and he'd recognized her. One of his boys told him about Poupelle and Poupelle's "love" racket, and Norman had started getting the germ of his idea. While he talked, one of the officers scribbled in a notebook. It seemed unreal to watch him writing while that twisted voice spoke, faltered, went on again.

"All of it was my idea," Norman said. "Whole thing. Hooks in Poupelle, had him where he'd do anything . . . even get married. He was smooth enough to work it. I needed money bad, knew I could get it from Poupelle once he had it. All I had to do was make sure he got it." He was talking fast, leaving out big parts of it, but they were easy to fill in. "Hooked him first with a rigged roulette wheel. Then Bender helped. Yates . . . had to be killed. He'd told me the girl was at Fairview."

He stopped for long seconds, then went on: "I hadn't known about the girl, just meant to kill the old lady, but that changed it. Made it . . . better, would look more like the old gal really banged herself. Be rid of both of them. Yates . . . he'd have known, afterward. Couldn't afford what he'd do. He'd double-crossed her already."

I said, "Who killed Yates?"

"Mike Hawkins. At the camp. Day after Yates's report about the daughter, I sent Mike there. Him and his wife. Saturday night I phoned Yates, had him take his own rifle out to Mike. Mike used it on him right there, that night. Oh, Jesus."

His face twitched. His eyes closed, then opened slowly. He said, his voice faint, "Scott?"

"Yeah."

"Scott, I sent Garlic out to your car, to blast you after you left the Redstone place. Mike was in camp right then, supposed to kill the girl that night, the gas . . . I hadn't heard from him. Knew the old gal must have hired you. Couldn't have you around messing things up, it was too close. I was jumpy. Mike had already missed getting the girl once. If I heard from him she was dead, I meant to kill the old lady that night."

He paused, blinking slowly, his mouth open, then went on. "Mike messed up both tries on the girl and I gave up on her — you were in it by then. Next night when you came out to the club I'd already given the story about the girl, and the pictures, to the *Clarion* reporter. After that I couldn't wait, had to do it later that night when the papers hit the street. I kept Poupelle and his wife, some other people, in the club. Andon stayed in my office while I went out the back way. He waited till I got back, then he told everybody we'd been together in the office. I went into town, got one of the newspapers and took it along, killed the old lady."

His voice was fainter now, but I could still hear him. "Andon had told me where her gun was. She knew I was going to kill her. Didn't try anything, just sat there. She just sat there. Didn't say a word. I . . . almost didn't do it."

He was silent then for what seemed a long time. When he looked at me his eyes were blank, dead-looking. His voice was a whisper. "Sorry I killed the old lady."

"That helps a lot, Norman."

Those were the last words he heard before he went out. He settled down on his elbow, then went the rest of the way to the ground. His hands fell slowly away from his stomach.

Laurel and I lay on the warm sand, hot sun burning our bodies an even deeper brown.

It was long after Norman had died. When his body had been hauled away I'd gone with Samson and the police to Fairview. Two of the hoods had been there, not quite knowing where to go without clothing. At least I'd burned up their clothes, even if I hadn't meant to do it. Foo, Babe, and one of the other brown-hooded couples had taken off for the hills, but they hadn't been hard to find. Not clad as they were in leaves and twigs.

Mr. and Mrs. Bob Brown — actually Mr. and Mrs. Mike Hawkins — had finally been picked up and were in the can. A large number of other criminal types were out of circulation. And Sergeant Billings had told me I didn't have to shoot anybody to make us even — I'd introduced him to Peggy. The last time I saw him, he was almost as tanned as she was. He could still blush, though. Carlos, I presumed, was still dancing with Juanita.

Andon Poupelle, not the strongest character I'd ever met, cracked during his first night in the poky and admitted he'd known about Norman's plans to murder Mrs. Redstone. Consequently he was an accessory before the fact, after the fact, and smack in the middle of the fact — smack in the middle of San Quentin, too, now.

Vera was in Las Vegas getting a divorce — since, among other things, the knowledge that Poupelle's proposal had been Norman's idea had annoyed her quite a bit — and simultaneously appearing in the show at the Sahara for

$10,000 a week, which she didn't need. Everybody even remotely connected with the case was famous.

Except me. I was infamous. But my sentence had been suspended and I was with Laurel, and life was good. I'd never been so bronzed and healthy in my life. Or so full of yeast and wheat germ. Besides, I'd never had my own nudist camp, total membership two people. It had to be my own. I had been banned from every nudist camp in the United States.

There had, of course, been quite a hullabaloo. I had been charged with everything from ballooning without a license to invading the planet, and other things too horrible to mention. One waggish idiot even had the gall to accuse me of being a press agent for the American Sunbathing Association. Arson, I think, was another charge. Oh, they got a lot of charges out of me. Anyway, Fairview had been insured. But that was all behind me now.

Laurel rolled over close to me, picked up a handful of white sand, and let it trickle onto my chest. Then she leaned even closer and whispered in my ear.

"No," I said. "Thank you, no. Not that the thought doesn't appeal to me. It's just impossible. Ha-ha."

"Oh, you can do anything."

"No. Some things I can't do. Really I can't."

Sunlight glinted on that soft hair, hair like copper and brass melted together, and her bright blue eyes were merry. "I'll give you a million dollars."

I stifled an imaginary yawn. It was a little gag of hers.

"Oh, all right," I said pettishly. "You and your damned money."

Quite a while later I said in a weak voice, "Well, I guess you're about broke by now. I hope to hell you're broke. We'll figure it up later. What will you do when you're a pauper?"

Laurel smiled beautifully, sleepily. "Oh, I'll think of something."

I knew she would. She always did. But naturally I wouldn't really take any of her money. It was enough that we were together, enjoying today and looking forward to tomorrow. It was enough that we were here, on a secluded beach in Hawaii.

Hell, yes. Hawaii.

THE END
of a Gold Medal Original by
Richard S. Prather

About the Author

RICHARD PRATHER is the author of the world famous Shell Scott detective series, which has over 40,000,000 copies in print in the U.S. and many millions more in hundreds of foreign-language editions. In 1986 he was awarded the Private Eye Writers of America's Life Achievement Award for his contributions to the Private Eyes Genre. He and his wife, Tina, live among the beautiful Red Rocks of Sedona, Arizona. He enjoys organic gardening, gin on the rocks, and golf. He collects books on several different life-enriching subjects and occasionally re-reads his own books with huge enjoyment, especially STRIP FOR MURDER.

Printed in the United States
80505LV00002B/59